SEER'S FORTUNE

Seer's Trilogy

Teresa Vanderhoof

Dedicated to Edwin, June, Leona, Bud, Bob, and Donna. I lova you.

CONTENTS

Title Page

Dedication

Chapter 1: The Temple   1

Chapter 2: The Centre   65

Chapter 3: Infirmary   84

Chapter 4: Great Council of Seers   98

Chapter 5: The Political House   118

Chapter 6: Quadrant Twenty-Four   146

Chapter 7: The Outer Ridge   176

Chapter 8: Herbalist   197

Chapter 9: The City   221

Chapter 10: The Barrens   256

Chapter 11: Home   280

Epilogue   295

Acknowledgement   303

About The Author   305

Books In This Series   307

The Communities

CHAPTER 1: THE TEMPLE

"There are no winners in war," or, at least that was what my grandmother used to say, "just those who lose less than others." This thought returned to me as I watched the series of animated Seer's history flicker before my eyes. Inky dark smoke rose in the distance as the crowd gazed upon the horizon of what was once known as Medietas, the original Capital of our ancestors. Children whimpered around me. I bit my lower lip keeping back the sniffles. I felt my Father's reassuring hand press upon my shoulder, and I edged closer to him. A round object was thrown into the square in front of us, exploding into deafening fragments. I saw men and women with an embroidered symbol upon the collar of their shirts. One came close to the crowd. I could distinguish the elaborate P with arrows swooping around it and a four-pointed star framing the symbol. These were the Preservationists. Another bomb was lobbed at a nearby tall building and glass rained down upon the stunned onlookers. Most were civilians who were caught up in the war. The Preservationists threw their arms out trying to protect the onlookers. In the cloud of dust and smoke I could make out men whose hair looked clumped together with clay. They wore necklaces of teeth from animals such as tigers and other feral creatures. They bared their yellow stained teeth at the frozen crowd. There were screams emanating from the sea of people and then panic tore them away from the site of the menace storming into their city. They fled, chaos bursting forth at manic speed. The brave Preservationists coaxed the fleeing people to side streets and away from the center of the fray. My own feet were at the ready to sprint away. The light touch of my Mother placing her hand on my other shoulder reminded me I was simply watching a projected holo of the events which shaped our current lifestyle and not within the destruction which lay before us. A line of guardians came forward with energy shields strapped to their arms and guns at the ready. The Nomads who brought forth the war upon Medietas pushed forward, determined to wipe out any who stood in their way. I was confused by what followed as bullets exploded against the shields throwing bright sparks. I had to look away. I could tell they were from the Nomads. I could hear the Preservationists retaliate but I couldn't see much of the fighting. I involuntarily shrank against my parents as another explosive destroyed another building. I saw people scrambling away as bricks tumbled down from above.

"That's the last of them, fall back!" I heard someone shout. Those who wiped bricks off their shields, which were now a dim flicker of light, ran as fast as they could. A hover tram pulled up alongside one of the severely damaged buildings. Those who had been running changed their course heading for the tram. A hand reached out to several people, pulling them onto the vehicle.

"We must go, now!" I heard someone yell at the driver. Those who had made it onboard jerked forward, almost falling off of the tram. They lurched into the void between two buildings whose only structure left standing was a broken skeleton core. A few who were left behind sank to their knees, knowing what was to come. A sudden boom consumed the area and was immediately followed by an ear-piercing silence. I was disoriented and clasped at my ears.

My Dad knelt beside me and whispered, "It's okay sweetheart." He kissed my forehead and stood back up. A roar filled the air and then nothing. The holo ended. The abruptness of the ending made me feel a bit dizzy. I was determined to stand tall beside my parents.

"We will never forget those who were left behind," the Senior Seer looked around at the awestruck crowd. "We will never again give in to destruction which took place that day." There was a murmured consent amongst the adults, the children unusually quiet.

"Retaliation, fighting, killing, these things lead us to the pinnacle of The Great War. This," he waved his hand and a new holo appeared before us, "is what compromise and peace can create."

A lone man strode away from the fighting, disappearing into mountains miles from the old Capital. The image blurred. When he returned, we could see him standing outside a cavern. In his hand was a mysterious, deep blue stone. The stone had a pulse of its own, like a heartbeat. I couldn't remember his name. I tried to think back to the history lessons we had last year. Was his name Erin? Ernie?

I heard an elderly woman beside us mutter, "Erik," saying his name in awe. Many spoke his name in this manner whenever they spoke of the original Seer of The Communities. I looked back up to the holo. He strode away from the mountains and headed to a temporary settlement to the north of the Capital ruins. Land was scorched and bits of vegetation was rotting on the ground. As he approached the small, temporary settlement guards rushed out to meet him.

"Halt!" They commanded.

Erik pulled back the fibrous hood which protected his head from the harsh elements. "I'm not here for war," his voice was soothing.

"Where do your allegiances lie?" A guard demanded.

"To peace," Erik replied smoothly.

The guards looked at each other, a bit timid at his response. Erik closed his eyes, seconds passing by before he responded. "I just want the best for our people," he seemed to choose his words carefully. It wouldn't be until later that the truth came out. I recalled that bit from my teacher's lesson. I remembered Erik would go on to tell the leaders who fled from the Capital the truth. He had obtained some strange ability. Erik said he could see the past, present, and future. He had been using this strange skill to negotiate with the Nomads and had got them to agree to a meeting with the survivors of the Preservationists to find compromise. They had agreed. After months of negotiation and careful planning Erik had succeeded where everyone else had failed. He reached a tentative peace. The Preservationists and all those who wanted to join them would take up residence in the north east corner of the world. The rest of the world would be left to the Nomads to live as they saw fit.

The image changed. A group of Seers stood

in a circle around the site, which was now our home, The Communities. Scientists joined them and placed a pole within the ground. A field grew from the poles and surrounded the area, placing a type of protection circle from the radiation which pressed down upon those who were on the outside. The holo zoomed to the inside of this protection. Although I knew I was not standing there I felt refreshed and at peace. The rail system was constructed before our very eyes with elapsed time speeding us forward. Farms were raised and sectors formed until it brought us to the center of our life, the Seer Temple. Here, it stood majestic before us. The wooden door looked smooth and inviting. The deep blue of the Seer Stone fixed at the very top of the door. My eyes followed the gold Fatras lines up the building past a multitude of stained-glass pieces stretching upward towards the heavens. At the top was the multi-hued stain glass dome. This grand place was the heart of our society. Here, the Elders of the Seer Guild met to discuss the fate of our community. Their decisions had kept the peace for us for many years. The holo ended again and in its place standing before the crowd were the current Elder members who ran the Seer Temple. Our saviors. I looked around and saw children and parents smiling up at the Elders. I wouldn't want everyone staring at me. That's why they were the Elders. They were our leaders. I kicked at a pebble on the ground and my Mother shushed me.

"People of The Communities," Elder Jaemson stood before the crowd. "We have come a long way in making our world a better place." There was a smattering of applause. "The Nomads destroyed our home. The fighting ensured the destruction of our world. However, we remain strong and proud of what we have accomplished here. As we celebrate the annual Seer Festival let us remember what we have lost."

"Let us remember," the adults in the crowd echoed.

Every year my parents would take me to the annual Seer Festival close to the center of The Communities, the city of Kastor. Colorful banners strung across halogen lamp posts and confetti peppered the sky. Vac bots continuously swept the streets, so nothing was littered upon the smoothly paved ground. The opening ceremony commemorated those who fought in the Great War while the festivities celebrated the accomplishments of those who worked hard to improve our life and our world. This was the first year I actually paid attention to the holo as I was now eight years old. However, that was as far as my attention went. I didn't really care about all the talking from the Elders and Senior Seers. I felt more connected to the images than in years past. Younger children were already pulling at their parents' hands, trying to get at the colorful balloons and the smells of thickly sweet sugar. Stalls were opening and the celebrations began.

My Father knelt beside me, "Don't wander away from your Mother," he warned me. "Make sure you can see her while you guys are looking around."

"When is your presentation Father?" I smiled at him. "In a couple hours," he smiled widely at me.

He slipped a small electronic chip into my hand, "For any sweets you want," he hugged me.

My Mother audibly sighed but then was laughing with us. "See you in a while," she gave Father a kiss.

"Yuck," I stuck out my tongue.

"You better think yuck for a very long time," Mother took my hand.

We walked amongst the food stalls. I chose the stickiest sweet I could find. I had it all over my fingers. I spent the next hour licking them as we walked from booth to booth. Some of the booths had designer clothes while others sold everyday household items to better improve the upkeep of your home. I wasn't interested in either, so I preoccupied my time licking the sweet goodness. Mother tapped on the band on her wrist and then tugged on my hand, directing me to the pavilion at the far end of the square. A banner above the staging area read "Today's future". Dad was set up on the stage. The board beside the stage read, "Staltech Quadrant 12". Mother found us seats close to the front of the stage. I sat kicking my feet back and forth underneath my chair. Father nervously smiled at us. His eyes flickered to the half-filled seats.

"Good morning everyone and welcome to Staltech Technology," he hit a button on his tablet. A screen came down and a short presentation began on the development of a new Tablet series which could act as a communicator, note taker, and connect to any network. My head jerked down as I began to sink into a sugar overdose coma. I felt my Mother put her arms around me and pull me into her lap. I could feel the evenness of her breathing and sank further into slumber.

I awoke later as the train rumbled into familiar territory, Quadrant 12. I could see the trees in the distance encircling our Quadrant and obscuring my vision of the train line. I was huddled in my Father's lap. He lifted me gently and my parents exited off the train.

"Should we grab something to eat before we head home, or should we just head back?" Father looked up and down the street. I opened my eyes, my vision a bit hazy from being so sleepy. I saw a golden line snake towards our house and an angry, throbbing red line towards the merchant section. I shook my head and said, "Home". I heard my Father giggle. "She is wiped out."

"To be honest I don't feel like cooking," Mother was looking around.

"Home," I urged.

"We will get there honey," Father tried to reassure me.

"No," I began to cry. "I want to go home," I insisted.

"What's wrong?" Mother looked at me with concern. I couldn't explain it. I was afraid of the monstrous line leading to the merchant district. I wanted nothing to do with it. "I just want to go home," I began to wail.

"Alright, alright," Father sighed. "There's no need for dramatics. I guess it was a long day."

I saw my Mother shrug and she rubbed my back soothingly. I knuckled at my eyes, wiping away the tears and smudging my face with sticky dirt which had collected on my sugary fingers earlier in the day. We heard an explosion behind us. Dad swung around. I couldn't see what was going on as I was still being carried by him. I could hear screams in the background.

"Take Pandria and head home. I'm going to help."

I felt myself being gently put to the ground. "Be a good girl and listen to your Mother," Father's gaze was at the inferno in the distance. I bit my lower lip and reached out for Mother's hand. She tentatively grabbed it as we both watched Father race towards the merchant district. I no longer saw the red, fire line that led to the merchant district. I did see the flow of firefighters and volunteers racing to put out the fire. We would have been a part of the accident had we gone out to dinner before heading home.

Mother pulled on my hand and led me on to our house. My head was turned to watch the flickering of lights grow smaller in the distance. I hoped no one was seriously injured. I wanted Dad to come home quickly.

Later in the night as I lay in bed, snuggled in my feather down, I could hear the front door creak open and close. I saw between the cracks of my slightly ajar door Mother's shadow pass in front of the lamp which glowed warmly in the corner of the living room.

"Are you okay," I heard Mother's hushed tones.

"Yes dear, I'm fine," I heard Father's voice, a bit gravellier than it was earlier in the night.

"Is Pandria in bed?" I could see him hugging her.

"Yes," I heard her muffled voice. He released her after a few short moments. "Is everyone else okay?" she tilted her head up to him.

He didn't respond. I squinted my eyes to try to see them better in the low light. He was shaking his head no.

"Do you think she knew?" Father looked intently at Mother. "Do you think she used the gift to see the danger?"

"I don't know," Mother looked towards my door. I shut my eyes tight. "We'll have to wait and see."

Father hugged her tightly again and then they padded off quietly to their room. I heard the door snick shut and I rolled over, staring at my wall. I had a feeling I knew what Father was asking. He was probably wondering if I had displayed the talent of the Seers. I wondered what it would be like, being a part of the great Temple in the middle. I recalled the holo I had seen earlier. Everyone staring at the Seers expecting great things from them; having to lead people away from destruction and despair. I didn't want that kind of responsibility. I just wanted to continue being me, learning science from my parents. I took a deep breath and let it out slowly the way

Mother had been showing me any time I was upset. I seemed to be getting upset more often these days. I had troubling dreams as I tossed and turned, trying to forget the red line which brought destruction to the merchant guild.

Months passed after this incident. My parents looked at me with concern. With no further development I noticed their glances became more relaxed and natural like the way we were before the Seer Festival. As they relaxed, so did I. I went to Academia in Quadrant 12. I was in my third year. I was still learning the basics of reading, writing, math, science, and history. I really wanted to turn my focus to the sciences. I loved to watch my Mother work in our herbal garden. I sat in the patch of the last of the fall sun breathing in the deep earthy perfume and the smell of rosemary filling my lungs.

"Hand me the shovel darling," Mother glanced over at me. I leaned over and reached the small hand shovel. "What's that on your hand?" Mother took my small hand in her larger one.

I stared at the scratch across the top of my hand. "It's nothing," I pulled my shirt sleeve up to try to cover it up. Mother just stared at me until I relented. "Fine," I huffed. "It was just Darla getting mad at me during break."

"She scratched you?"

"She didn't mean to," I tried to brush off the encounter.

"Did you tell your teacher?" Mother scowled at me.

"No, I can take care of it. It was just a mis-understanding," I insisted. I tried to redirect her attention by asking her about the garden, "Do we need to bring in the lavender over the winter months. I don't want them to freeze."

Mother pondered, "No, we will just need to make sure it has enough mulch to make sure it doesn't become over soaked during the rainy sea-son. Now, stop trying to change the subject. Why did Darla get mad at you?"

I picked at a dirt spot on my fingers before saying, "She was picking on another girl. I didn't like it. I refused to join her in making fun of her. Darla got mad at me."

"Did you tell the teacher Darla was being a bully?" Mother looked sideways at me.

"No," I stretched out the 'o'.

Mother set down the hand shovel and turned my head towards her. "I'm proud you didn't par-ticipate in bullying another student. However, sometimes not doing anything about it can be just as hurtful as participating in the bullying.

You should have told an adult about the bullying. Sometimes we need to stand up for what is right even if it is not easy."

I nodded and bit my lower lip.

"I'm not mad at your Pandria. Think of this as a learning experience." I nodded and tried to give her a smile. She smiled back and then changed the subject back to the plants we were tending to.

The next day shone bright as most of the clouds had temporarily cleared from the wind last night. I saw Darla at the front of the school pushing another girl. I took a deep breath and then set myself to face her. Before I could take a step, a golden thread wound in front of me. I paused, frozen in my tracks. To the side of the girls heading off to the playground where the other kids were waiting for school to begin was a red line. Into the school was a dark ebbing line pulsating. I was scared. If it weren't for the inviting golden line, I didn't think I would have had the bravery to walk up to Darla. I recalled Mother's words from the night before,

"Sometimes we need to stand up for what is right even if it isn't easy." I swallowed down the fear trying to beat out of my chest. I walked up to Darla and the girl she was bullying.

"Darla, give it a rest," I squared myself against her.

"Oh, Pandria," she mocked. "I'm scared now."

"When did you become an annoying bully?" I crossed my arms.

"Leave it," I heard the girl whisper.

"Darla, what you're doing is wrong."

"Come off it Pandria and leave this to the big girls," Darla snidely said through pursed lips.

"Being a bully doesn't make you a big girl."

"It's one thing to refuse to help me," Darla spat, "but it's something else to stand against me."

"Someone needs to," I retorted.

"What's going on here?" I recognized the voice of Master Catherine.

"Nothing Mam," Darla said sweetly.

"Not nothing," I grumbled.

Again, the girl who was cowering beside me said, "Leave it."

The golden light became brighter and emanated from the teacher, "I can't," I glanced at the girl I was standing up for. "Sometimes we have to stand up for what is right even if it involves someone who is my friend."

"Used to be," I heard Darla growl.

I clenched my teeth and forced the tears which burned at the side of my eyes to subside, "Darla was bullying Marison. She's been making fun of her a lot lately."

"Well?" Master Catherine looked coolly at Darla.

"We were just talking, weren't we Mary?" Darla scowled at the girl.

"No, you weren't," I persisted. "She is lying Master."

Master Catherine looked at Marison, "It's okay, you can tell me the truth. You won't get in trouble." Reluctantly Marison nodded in agreement with me.

"Darla, come with me," Master Catherine pointed into the school.

Darla kicked a pebble towards me and then stormed into the building. "Traitor," I heard her hiss as she whipped past us.

"Why did you do that?" Marison's small voice quavered. "She's going to be more horrible the next time I see her."

"She needs to learn it's not okay to be a bully," I sheepishly said. I knew my heart was in the right place. I was so nervous as I was speaking to Marison. I didn't want to be labeled a tattletale. I closed my eyes and saw some options before me. If I told her I was doing what was right I could see a red line surround that option. If I choose to let her know my Mother insisted I stand up to a bully, I saw a black void. A third option appeared before me. I could let her know I wanted to be her friend and a good friend would never let someone bully them. I opened my eyes. To me, the moment of decision seemed like an eternity. To Marison it was only a second. I decided to trust my gut instinct, "I wanted to be your friend, Marison. And friends stand up for each other."

"You," Marison pointed hesitantly at me, "want to be friends with me?"

"Yes," I tried to sound convincing. The answer felt right to me, like a piece of the puzzle fitting perfectly. "I want to be your friend."

A small smile started to spread across Marison's face. "Okay," Marison said shyly.

The bell gonged deep within the school and we all filtered into the school. We didn't see Darla until after lunch. She glared openly at me but didn't say a word to either myself or Marison. I ran home as soon as the last bell gonged and darted into the kitchen. I could smell blueberries being baked in the oven. Mother was cooking blueberry muffins. I inhaled deeply.

"Hello sweetheart," Mother said cheerfully. "How was your day."

I peeked into the oven and Mother shooed me away. "It was okay," I sat on a stool to stare eagerly at the oven.

"Did you take care of the problem you were having yesterday?"

"Yes," my gaze dropped to the floor.

"Was she picking on you too?" Mother leaned on the counter close to me.

"No, she was picking on the same student again. I told Master Catherine what Darla was doing. Darla hates me now," a tear slid down my cheek.

Mother picked up a cloth and wiped away my tears, "You did the right thing," Mother smiled at me.

"Mom," I tapped a finger on the counter, "I didn't know what to tell Marison after Darla was taken inside. She wasn't happy I stood up for her. She was afraid I would have made things worse for her. I saw lines which told me what I should say to her."

"Lines?" Mother looked at me quizzically.

"Different choices," I tried to explain. Mother

looked more confused and quietly waited for me to finish. "I thought if I told her you told me I should do the right thing she would have gotten mad. She didn't really want adults involved. Instead, I told her I wanted to be her friend. That wasn't my plan when I confronted Darla. Things just ended up with us agreeing to be friends."

"We all have difficult choices sometimes. We often don't know what the consequences of those choices are going to be," Mother looked intently at me.

"Yea, that's it," I nodded in agreement.

Mother looked a bit disappointed for some reason. The look was gone the next second. We heard a ding and I hopped off my chair. Mother pulled out the muffins and pried one loose for me.

"Thank you," I grinned. I took the muffin and my book bag to my room, nibbling at the edges of the hot muffin until the rest of it cooled.

Hours later I heard Dad come through the door. I smiled as I peeked out to see my parents embracing each other. I heard Mother whisper. I couldn't make out the words. Father replied, "More of a life lesson than the gift, then?"

"I believe so," Mother replied. They went into the kitchen where I heard pots and pans being dragged from their hiding places in the cupboard.

Little episodes like this happened on occasion over the next year. By the time I was nine I began to trust the lines which spread out before me. Every time my Mother and Father caught me at this, they would look excited and hopeful. I just wanted them to be proud of me. I didn't want some special ability that would bring unwanted attention from the entire Community. I found myself talking more to Marison about the strange lines than I did my own parents. I made her promise not to say anything to anyone. After I helped her with Darla, I became her friend. Marison was willing to keep my secrets. Marison had confided in me she didn't want to follow in her Mother's footsteps and become a herbologist. I kept her secret and she was happy to keep mine. Many students chose to specialize in the same areas as their parents.

"How can you not want acknowledgement if you were a Seer?" Marisol poked at my arm one day. We were sitting out in a field of daisies while the other kids were playing games.

I pointed to a boy who was several years ahead of us. He was joking with his friends as they kicked a ball back and forth. "He told the teachers and his parents about his talents as a Seer. They took him to The Temple and now he is leaving in a few days to join the Seers. He is leaving behind his friends and family here. Sounds lonely. Besides, can you see them all gushing over him. He can never get any peace. People will always be bothering him about his 'gift'".

"You're strange, you know that, right?" Marisol laughed. I threw a bunch of daisies at her instigating a flower fight.

As I laid in bed that night, I pondered Marisol's words. Was I really strange and different from other people? There had to be others out there who just wanted to live a normal, quiet life. My Mother and Father seemed content with their quiet lives. I wanted to be just like Mother, a botanist. I loved the smell of dirt and enjoyed digging my fingers into the rich soil. I didn't understand all the testing my Mother had done to the earth or the plants. I wanted to learn what it all meant. I saw the beauty in every moss, leaf, and delicate stem. I loved how the light shone through the leaves of a rose bush or the glistening dew drops in the morning, clinging to every blade of grass. I glanced out my window and saw a fresh sky with shimmering lights winking in the velvet sky. I loved how they twinkled in the night sky.

I was sitting outside, tending to the berry bushes in front of our house. I saw a burnt, fiery red line stretching out before me, a blackened void dart to the left, and an iridescent glow to the right. The webbed lines stretched out before me. I was the only one here as Mother and Father were inside cleaning the house. I was confused as to why I was seeing this now. Was I in danger? Then I saw it, a ghost of a boy no older than five was chasing a toy across the train tracks. I suppressed a scream as the boy didn't clear the track in time. The image disappeared. Tears slid down my cheek. I scrambled to my feet trying to understand what I just saw. The image I had seen was like a holo. The image had disappeared as fast as it had appeared. I looked around, there was no one in sight. I shook my head trying to rid myself of what I just saw. Then a boy stumbled from behind his house, a red ball bouncing away from him. The boy started chasing after the ball. I sprinted for the boy. He bent down and hobbled towards the ball, and the train tracks. I bowled into him. We landed in a tangled mess on the ground. The boy beat at me trying to get back up to chase his ball. We watched as his ball rolled across the tracks and the train plowed over it. I heard a woman's scream and looked back towards the houses, realizing the scream I heard must have be his mother. She rushed over to us, staring at the train as it sped by. Mother and Father were running towards us as well. Father's mouth was open. Mother just looked intently at me.

"You made me lose my ball," the five-year-old

tried to kick me. His Mother scooped him up in her arms.

"Timothy Matthew how dare you get mad at this young lady!" his Mother scolded him. "If she hadn't stopped you, you would be as flat as your ball."

"But my ball," he sobbed.

"Are you okay Pandria?" Father hugged me tightly. I hadn't realized he had reached me already. I closed my eyes tight as he held me close. I guess my secret wasn't so secret anymore.

"Yes, I murmured into his dusty sweater."

"Honey, what happened?" Mother crouched down beside me.

"I saw it all from my front window, Mrs. Arturas," the woman interrupted. "I saw her weeding the bushes. She looked off into the distance like The Seers at The Temple do. The next thing I know I saw my Timothy running towards the tracks. She stopped him," tears glistened in her eyes. "You saved my son. Thank you so much!"

I nodded to her, not knowing what to say. I didn't want the attention. I was happy the boy was safe. I wasn't happy she was paying so much attention to me. "You're welcome," I shyly replied.

"Darling," Mother turned me to face her. "Did you see the future before it happened?"

I tried not to look her in the eyes and searched around for some reasonable excuse to give her. My mind was numb and blank. I finally ended up just shaking my head yes. I bit my lip.

"You're not in trouble, honey," Father looked concerned.

"I know," I said.

"I think she's in shock," Mother said to the other woman. "I'm glad your son is okay."

"If there is anything, we can do for you guys please let me know and thank you again!" She smiled widely at me.

Father steered me back inside. It was then I realized how much dirt was sticking to my fingers. I wiped them absently on my pants. Mother was beaming and chattering about this gift was a great fortune. She didn't chastise me for getting my pants filthy. She didn't mind dirt. I was caking the dirt on my pants. She sat me down on the couch and sat beside me. She began talking about going to our local Political House to find the local resident Seer to have them test my skills. My mind wandered away from her jabbering. I replayed the events in my head. If I had ignored the vision Timothy would have died in front of me. I didn't want that. I had never seen anyone die. When my Grandmother was ill, she passed away at the Herbalist Building. My parents had shielded me from her death the best they could. I felt her absence. I was glad I didn't have to witness her dying from the illness she had got somehow. I knew letting the kid run into the tracks hadn't been an option. My parents taught me to do what was right no matter the cost. I remembered the iridescent line. I wondered what would have happened had I chosen the line. I had unconsciously chosen the black void line. I wasn't sure what this meant. My heart constricted and for the first time in a while I was afraid.

I spent the next six months with the Seer at the Political House. They gave me a series of tests. At home I was screaming in the night. I woke up with sweat pouring down my face, my hands twisting the sheets of my bed. Mother and Father were alarmed by this development. They even took me to see the herbologist. She gave my Mother some sleeping serum to help me sleep at night. My nightmares lessened a bit. Still, there were some nights I lay awake with fear gripping my heart. I couldn't explain it and I couldn't remember my nightmares. I looked out at the school field, Marisol sitting quietly beside me. I didn't see the daisies like I had prior to having the vision. They were blurred white blobs upon the field. What Seers didn't tell the common folk was your vision of the world would be changed forever. The beauty of it all took a backseat to the multitude of lines which crisscrossed from each person and thing from within our culture. The original Seer may have stopped the fight over politics, religion, and ideals but there was a price to the gift normal people would never understand. The Communities may strive to develop a highly intellectual, reserved society but I didn't want to be a part of the Seers to accomplish this goal.

I turned ten and the testing from our local Seer was over. They had determined I was to be another student of the Seer Guild. My parents arranged to take me to The Temple to face the Elders of the Seers. I would have to face them before my final admittance to Seer training. The Temple was not an indication of a religious sect. In the distant past, before Kastor was destroyed, it would have been a place of worship. With the appearance of the Seers, it was now a place to test promising disciples of the Select Seer Group. Governors were still in charge of the local every day running of The Communities. The Seers kept the peace, preventing most problems before they arose. Minor crimes were still committed. There was a police force. There was no need for grand juries or large militant groups.

My parents dressed me up in a blue, frilly dress which was way beyond their pay grade. I was certain they would sacrifice a month's worth of food coupons to present me in style. They wanted me to look the part of an important Seer. I felt silly in the dress. I preferred pants and a shirt over anything with frills.

The train took us past Kastor and into the heart of The Communities. As we approached the Seer Temple rose like a hopeful beacon. The stained-glass windows refracted the light of the sun, throwing deep amber, forest greens, and other rich colors around the Seer campus. I heard Mom take a deep breath in at the sight of the tall building. We hopped off the train when it pulled into the station. Even though we were just at a train station it was still lavishly adorned. Swirls of gold swept across the floor and was embedded in a deep, purple granite floor.

Father looked down and whistled, "They sure are fancy here."

"It's beautiful," Mother slowly moved forward.

We moved on towards the entrance to the Seer Campus. A great archway invited us in. Once we crossed over, we saw an array of students and teachers walking around the campus. In the center stood tall the Seer Temple. We caught our first glimpse of the Wooden Oak door to the home of the Seer Elders. They would be the ones I had to stand before in order to receive my final approval to join the elite Seers. As we approached the door opened on its own. My parents joined me as we crossed over into a waiting room.

The walls and floors emitted a deep cold. They were made of a rare metal mined in the Outer Ridges. I looked up and could see the azure sky through the crystal ceiling. The Grand Hall opened up to a large, circular room. Throne-like chairs were melded around the perimeter of the room. My parents walked me between two of the grandiose chairs and to the center. I looked down and saw the metal had transitioned to glass with inlaid gold lines flowing away from the center and throughout the entire floor; just as my own vision had done for me leading me to The Seer Centre.

I noticed upon each chair sat a man or woman with eyes unlike any I had seen in normal society. I had heard the more a Seer looked at the lines of possible outcomes of destiny the more their eyes matched what they saw. The woman closest to us, whose hair shimmered white, had eyes of steel gray with broken lines of a lighter gray. I could tell she could see the lines which connected me to the possible, infinite choices of my future. I wondered what she saw and if it matched what I saw.

To the right of me the red-haired man spoke in a deep, distant voice, "You have come before us to present your child as a possible candidate to serve the Seers."

"We have, Great Seer," Father's voice echoed.

"Come forth, child," the woman's voice whispered.

I hesitantly stepped forward, bowing slightly as my parents showed me on the train here. "Peace, great Lady," I rigidly responded as taught from birth.

"Peace, Pandria," her voice whispered again. I looked up and noticed she was not speaking at all. The sound of her voice was being projected from her mind. This astonished me.

"What is it, child?" the red-haired man asked.

"I'm sorry, Great Seer," I stuttered. "I thought she was speaking to me. Her mouth is not moving," I crunched my brows together.

"Pandria!" Mother gasped. "Please, forgive her Great Seer. She means no offense."

"Pardon is not needed here, Mrs. Arturas," he turned his lined eyes upon me, "She is mute, child. She can only communicate with those who hold the potential."

"And I hold the potential?" I timidly asked.

"What do you think?"

I looked around and saw new lines break off

from the ones I saw coming into the circular room. To the left the void, to the middle a fiery red line, back the way we came in the path sparkled. The Great Seer followed my gaze. I looked up at his gray eyes. The lines I first saw flowed deeper into him and I felt mesmerized. Images ghosted at the corners of my vision: fires, buildings crumbling, and floods washing out forests. The rush of surmounting energy washed over me. I gasped for breath.

From the last thread of light before my vision blackened, I saw Mother rush to my side. Father cried out in despair.

My head burned violently. My eyes watered each time I tried to open them. Etched into my field of vision I could see golden threads like the floor of the Seer's Temple. I screamed and clawed at my eyes. Gentle hands entrapped my own and a soft, cool cloth was wrapped around my head. "Rest now," the soft whispering voice said. The soothing cadence of her voice wrapped around my consciousness. I went back into the blackened unknown.

When I woke again, I couldn't tell the time. All I could see was a watery darkness from the cloth which was still wrapped around my head. I could hear the familiar hum of my Mother's voice as she sang my favorite lullaby. I recalled when I started having the vicious nightmares, she would sing to me. Her songs were the only thing which would soothe me back to a peaceful sleep. She was humming one of the songs now.

"Mother," my cracked voice reached out to her.

"Here, Pandria," I felt the warmth of her fingers wrap around my own.

"Is Father here, too?"

"He's making arrangements for us to have temporary lodging while we are in the heart of The Communities," she began humming again.

"Why?" I asked. "We can leave now. I feel much better." I noticed Mother had abruptly stopped humming. "What is it?" my lips quivered.

"Nothing, darling," Mother smoothly wiped a hand down my cheek. Tears were seeping from beneath the cloth.

"Please, don't lie to me," my voice shook. "What is wrong with me?"

"They say it's probably nothing and happens from time to time," Mother tried to reassure me.

"What aren't you telling me?" my fist clenched against her fingers.

"You have seen more deeply than any other, child. The effects are powerful and unpredictable," the whispering voice answered for Mother.

"What will happen to me?" I asked aloud.

"I'm not sure what Master Kinnet has said to you Pandria. The doctors have said they are unsure. You could be just fine in the next day or two or you could be. . .," Mother's voice broke.

"Tell me the truth," panic rose in my voice.

"You might become blind," I heard Father's deep voice respond for Mother who was sobbing.

"That's what happened to you, is-n-it?" I asked to the unknown voice.

There was a pause before she answered, "Yes."

I turned my head away from both of them, only guessing where I thought they would be. "I want to be alone," I swallowed hard.

"Pandria, don't be silly. I'm not leaving my daughter alone," Mother's voice came across a little harsh.

"Leave, please," my voice dripped with anger. I could feel the Seer's hand touch Mother's. The weight of her fingers left mine. I was alone with my despair.

I told the nurses I didn't want to see anyone. I think at the request of the mysterious voice I had heard in my head the nurses listened to me. This lasted for the next several days, or so I was guessing since I couldn't see. The Seers kept the cloth tightly bound around my eyes and only removed it to apply more soothing gel upon its surface. Whenever they took off the cloth, no matter how briefly, all I could see were the outlines of shapes and the multitude of lines which flowed from them. The tears I had shed for days were now unwilling to come. The sadness sunk to the depth beyond tears. Time became non-existent while I lay helplessly upon the bed. They had moved me to a new location since the episode in the Seer's Temple. The room they moved me to felt no different than where I was before. After days of refusing to let my parents anywhere near me the nurses told me they had enough and let them in anyway.

Father's smooth hand grabbed mine. "Don't think for one minute you are no longer our daughter. We love you, Pandria. These things have not changed."

"Refusing us was silly, Pandria." Mother began.

"Hush for now, Mother," Father's soft voice warned. "She is still young, after all."

I could imagine Mother biting her lip, keeping herself from berating me even further. There was no more talk after that. Just the breathing of my parents and the silent conversation I guessed they were having.

I was in and out of consciousness. The deep sleep was much better than the blackness I woke up to; only reminded me of my loss of sight. The Seers had been in, from the Seer Centre, to look upon me and try to assist with my recovery. The only one who brought me any measurable amount of comfort was the woman with no voice. She, too, had lost something for the thing which society deemed an honorable gift.

She had warned me not to become bitter. In bitterness the gift could turn inward and cause an insurmountable amount of pain and grief for everyone, including myself. In the Academy I remembered our science labs and how the professors stated for every action there was an opposite and equal reaction. I thought of what she said as akin to this lesson.

They were changing my cloth, as they usually did when I first woke up in the mornings, and it was then I began to see the first glimpses of real shapes. Not just their outlines. I gasped.

"Are you hurt?" Father rushed to my side. I lovingly looked up at him. For the first time in weeks saw the color of his eyes. After much blinking I was able to focus seeing the emerald color of his eyes. I touched his stubbly face. "Father," I cried.

"She can see!" he turned towards Mother.

Mother rushed to my other side. Both of my parents were hugging me tighter than they had ever before. I grasped onto them but kept my eyes open in fear of not being able to see again.

A parade of people visited me after this turn of events. Seer Masters, Elders, the nurses, and doctors all performed their own examinations on me. All came to the conclusion I would indeed keep my sight even if it was not the same as it was before. I no longer saw just objects and people. I saw golden lines running around and through whatever I saw. I was frustrated at first finding it difficult to concentrate to look past those lines. After weeks more working with the Seers I began to see past the lines. The mute Master Seer who can speak in my mind, Master Atheara Kinnet was the most helpful. She trained me to clear my mind. When she first entered the world of the Seers, she had been overwhelmed with the sounds of the world. Just as my eyesight was overwhelmed with the multitude of lines I saw.

They gave me the loose drab clothing of the potentials and moved me out of the hospital wing. My parents chose to return to our home after they were convinced, I was no longer in danger of forever losing my eyesight. They were going to receive a stipend for my training here, just as any other profession would. Most careers would only receive a small portion of food and lodging coupons. For Seers they offered only the best compensation. I bunked with other potentials. My own bed resided in the farthest corner of the large room, right next to a round crystal window. The Seer Centre had its own version of The Academy. Every morning we spent time with reading, writing, math, science, and other core skills. The afternoons were reserved solely for meditation and fine tuning our Seer skills.

The first day of classes was nerve wracking. I had started later than other potentials due to my time in the medical ward. An older student had gathered my basic supplies issued by the Centre. She handed me a bag and I could feel the thump of a tablet against my hip. She carried a pillow and some blankets in her arms as we headed to the dorms. We passed other girls who giggled. One girl with dark colored hair flicked her hair over her shoulder glaring at me as we walked by. Judging from the quality of her clothes and the high style tablet she carried in her arms it appeared she was from the Capital of Kastor. I looked down at the ground as we continued onto the dorms which lay to the farthest corner of the campus. We entered one set of doors and passed through a living quarter where some of the students were gathered, talking over various topics. Some of them were watching videos on their tablets while others looked to be studying from online texts. We wound our way up a set of stairs and entered a room which had four different beds. The older student set the stuff down on the bed closest to a crystal window.

"If you need anything else you can ask the dorm leader located on the first floor."

"Thank you," I said quietly.

She left. I sat down on my new bed. I looked out the crystal window and wondered what Mother and Father were doing. I rolled over and pulled out the tablet from the bag. I clicked it on and saw a welcome sign on it. After inputting login information, I saw my class schedules. In the mornings I was expected to attend the regular Academic topics while the afternoon was filled with classes specifically about Seers and how to use our abilities.

The next morning the sun rose brightly, watering down the colors of the blades of grass. I looked at the electronic map and followed it to my first classes. I managed not to get lost my first full day of school. I didn't manage to make any friends. I saw the snobby girl again. I tried to avoid her the best I could. I sat at the back of my classes and tried to keep my head down. By the end of my first week many of the kids were staring at me to get a glimpse of my eyes. My classmates still had the same-colored eyes they had when they entered the Centre. I did not. The stares bothered me, and I found myself finding secluded places to stay away from the others during our free time.

I walked across the campus eating a nutrition bar, heading towards my next class, History of the Seers. Master Barnsworth was fiddling with the projector at the front of the classroom. She absently waved at me as I headed towards my place at the back of the room. I shoved the last of the bar into my mouth as I pulled out my tablet from my bag. Other kids began to wander into the classroom. This class was bigger than our practicum classes. I watched as some girls from The City shooed away some Quad kids from some chairs they wanted. I tried not to roll my eyes. I had learned the leader of the snob girls was Kyra. She came from a privileged family and surrounded herself with superficial friends. I had only had the one true friend before coming to The Temple. I really didn't know how to go about introducing myself to others. I was the same way at the normal Academia. I was more interested in reading books out in the field while the other kids played. Here, I continued to do the same. I saw a lanky boy sit a few chairs ahead of me. He turned around and smiled at me. I ducked my head down and stared absently at my tablet. I was spared the awkward moment by Mrs. Barnsworth clearing her throat. Kyra and her gang mumbled. Then everyone quieted down. We were meant to be on our best behavior while at school here. We not only were the center of The Communities but representatives of our Quads and, essentially, our families. I had no interest in being the center of attention. I didn't want to disappoint my parents, either.

"Today, class, we are going to discuss the creation of The Temple." Barnsworth tapped a couple times on her tablet. The image flickered for a moment and then projected an image of The Temple. The multi-hued colors of glass sparkled out from the building. Golden lines intertwined as they flowed towards the sky. The huge oaken door stood tall. "Who can tell me what the jewel is at the top of the door?"

"It's the Seer's Fortune jewel Mam," one of Kyra's followers smirked.

"And who can tell me the significance of this jewel," Barnsworth continued.

A mousy haired boy next to Thomas raised his hand, "It was found by someone in The Communities?" He asked.

A few chuckles went around the room. Barnsworth wasn't deterred. "More specifically, Erin. How about you Pandria?" She looked at me with a small smile.

All eyes turned to look at me. A few gasps

went around me. This seemed to be the common reaction when they looked at the lines standing out in my eyes. I responded to Barnsworth's question to the desk. I was glad inanimate objects couldn't stare at me, "It was found by the first Seer. The stone held genetic altering properties."

"Very good Pandria," Barnsworth clicked to the next picture which showed the inside of The Temple. The chairs circled around the room for the Elders to sit in. I stared harder at the desk as I felt some eyes linger on me. I heard a shuffle of paper and a growl coming from Kyra. I looked up and saw the lanky boy had thrown a piece of wadded paper at her when Barnsworth's back was turned. She stuck out her tongue at him. The lanky boy dropped his hand below the level of the desk. He gave me a thumbs up so Kyra couldn't see him. I nodded at him as he glanced behind him. Kyra was no longer paying attention to me and was glaring at the board.

Days became weeks and weeks months as I trudged from one class to another. I had finally become accustomed to the stares whenever I entered a room. I simply bowed my head down and swiftly passed by everyone. I was tired of being the girl with the golden lined eyes.

I attended several classes a day. After breakfast I went to Master Kenneth's class who was lecturing us on the decay of radioactive particles. I dutifully took notes with those sitting in the back of the room. I could hear whispered conversations about our upcoming break. My mind screeched at them to shut up so I could hear better. Instead, I kept my mouth clamped shut so I wouldn't stand out in class.

"And how does this level of radiation react to the fatras, Pandria?"

"It makes it harder to discern the paths, obscuring our sight of the fatras, and can lead to incorrect readings," I almost whispered. Fortunately, my teachers had become accustomed to my quiet answers.

"Yes, and Kyra how high does the level of radiation need to be in order to completely obscure the fatras from our sight?"

"Sixty percent," Kyra answered in a loud voice then smirked at me.

This was how it was in many of my classes. There were plenty of classmates who ignored me all together once the Masters began to lecture. However, there were still those who felt intimidated by my presence in their class. Somehow, I had the impression they felt my weird colored eyes set me apart and oftentimes above them. This was not the case. I just put forth a lot of effort to excel in all the classes so I could leave the

Centre as soon as I could. I hated the stares I got from my fellow classmates.

The golden sun shone brightly through the window domed room which belonged to Master Gillath. All professors were considered Masters no matter their specialty.

"You all have a linear view of the threads of destiny, fatras. You can pluck these threads and hear their resounding lines echo as if a musician plucks the strings of a violin and hear the vibrations of the connecting strings. You can pull these strings forward to determine the destined future and then pull it back to see what the past could have been."

I listened intently to his words, using them to nourish my insatiable appetite.

"Don't think of the strings as just a trick of your sight but as living tangible objects. The normal person is not able to see these strings. Just because you cannot see something doesn't mean they aren't there."

"Why don't people accidently trip over these strings, then?" the Potential named Thomas looked up puzzled. I recognized him as the lanky boy from History class.

"Fatras are more than just an object, Thomas," Master Gillath smiled kindly at Thomas. "They are an essential part of our world and are interwoven with our lives flowing just as energy particles of light flow."

The other boys and girls laughed yet they still looked at Thomas intently. "You all laugh at his question, yes?" Master Gillath continued to smile. "Except you, Pandria."

"I thought his question was valid," I averted my eyes. I didn't like the attention.

"And why is that?" he encouraged.

"In order to understand we should always ask questions." I muttered.

"Very true, Potential Pandria, very true. You all would do well to think as Thomas does. Question everything."

A gong resounded in the distance. This indicated the end of another Seer session and the beginning of dinner. We rose from our spots on the ground and exited through the smooth metal door which slid open for us as we neared it. I hung back with Thomas.

"Thank you," he stared at the ground.

"For what?" I stared at him.

"Standing up for me," he glanced up and then rushed out the door.

I slowly followed after him, feeling the stare of

the Master behind me.

I walked quietly beside Thomas across the soft lawn. Our feet swooshing in the grass.

"What class do you have next?" Thomas hefted his bag higher on his shoulder.

I pulled out my tablet and tapped on it, "Leadership," I grumbled.

"You don't like the class?" he looked at me quizzically.

"I don't like the idea of being the center of attention," I mumbled.

"We are the leaders of today's society," he tried to mock Reese's low toned voice.

I looked intently at him trying to decide if he was making fun of me or trying to cheer me up. A grin broke across his face, "Sure thing Captain Thomas," I faked a salute.

We both laughed as we watched the long, brown haired city brat pass by us. She flicked her hair as she passed, hitting me across the face. I saw Thomas stare intently at her. I sighed and began walking again.

"What?" he hurried after me.

"Nothing," I stomped on.

"You don't have to worry about Kyra," he

watched as the girl ran up to her friends and whispered in their ear. "She may seem snobbish but she can be nice."

"I'll let you be nice to her then," I said. I left him at the door, staring after Kyra like a puppy who saw a bowl full of peanut butter.

I immediately took a place in the far back of the room closest to a window whose crystal panes broke up the light of the sun. I pulled out my tablet and set up for another class full of notes.

The afternoon spun by as we shuffled from one practicum class to another. I caught Thomas glancing at me a few times, attempting to make faces at me while no one was paying attention. When the final bell gonged, I shook my head and headed out the door.

"I think I made you smile that time," he whispered in my ear and then headed for the boys' dormitory.

I quickly ran to grab a meal before the rest of the students filtered in. I found a low-key location away from the center of the hub of students conversing about the day's lessons.

Meals were solemn affairs, each of us trying to synthesize the information they were throwing at us. There was a lot to take in. There were practical classes which required us to try to use our talents and then there were the theory sessions; each one more demanding than the next.

The classroom was cold. I shivered as I took my seat beside the window; the watery sunlight beating against the windowpane brought some warmth. Other students filtered into the classroom, speaking in low whispers. A few gave me a passing glance and sat as far back in the class as they could. I felt a pang of jealousy, straining to hear their whispered conversations. I thought I had heard one of them mention my name. They briefly looked up from their conversation. I bit my lip and quickly looked down at my desk, memorizing the wooden lines running through the surface. I heard the door creak open. An elderly woman hobbled into the classroom.

"Now class," her nasally voice echoed throughout the room. "Today we will be learning about the origins of the Seers," she brushed a thread of silver from her forehead. "Please take out your journals." Her back turned towards us as she flicked on a viewer behind her. The projection of the map of our world as it used to be filled the wall. "Many years ago, we were at war. Does anyone remember why?"

I saw every eye upon me, and my face burned. I knew the answer but had no ambition to answer. Finally, Thomas timidly raised his hand.

"Yes, um," she scanned the tablet in her hand. "Thomas."

"There were disputes over how to efficiently use the resources our world provided," he smoothly replied.

"Correct, Thomas."

I snuck a glance up and saw him warmly smile at me. I smiled back in appreciation but heard the giggle of the girls behind us. Thomas looked back at them and winked at one of the girls with long black hair. She blushed and hurriedly whispered to her friend.

Mrs. Caras scowled at the girls and then continued on, "Missy since you seem so keen to be chatty today why don't you tell us what the structure of our world was like during this time."

I saw Missy roll her eyes and glared at the blushing girl beside her, "There were the Preservationists who thought we were abusing our use of the resources. Opposite them were the Nomad Group who used up what they could in the area they were living before moving on."

"Kind of like vultures," Thomas slowly said.

The girls giggled again. The black-haired girl looked at him with curiosity. I rolled my eyes and looked back at the teacher.

Mrs. Caras ignored Thomas, "Yes," she nodded. She launched into the history of the War.

After class I tossed my journal into my bag along with my tablet. I tried to hurriedly exit but Thomas blocked my way.

"Leaving in a hurry?" he chuckled.

"I'm just trying to get to my next class," I stared at the floor. I tried to focus my attention on the flaws of the wood.

"Come on, I'm just trying to be friendly," he tried to catch my gaze.

I looked up at him and said, "Thanks for answering for me but I have to go." I pushed past him and practically ran to Math class. I could hear Missy gloating to her friend, "Kyra, I think she just jilted your new boyfriend," she elbowed her.

"Cut it out, Missy," Kyra slapped at her arm. Both girls balled up in a fit of laughter as I marched past them without a word.

The cafeteria was buzzing with the voices of students on their lunch break. I entered the food court, lifting a brown tray from the dish reciprocal. The fresh vegetable line was low, so I briskly walked over. After filling my plate, I scanned my card and headed to the farthest corner I could find. I sat down and flipped on my tablet looking over the morning's notes. A message beeped and I tapped the message.

"She's not my girlfriend," the message read. I looked up from a mouthful of lettuce and saw Thomas several tables away sitting with a group of good-looking boys. They all looked athletic, like they had spent most of their time playing sports rather than studying to be Seers.

I nodded to Thomas then went back to reading my notes. My tablet vibrated again. I tapped the message. "You know you don't have to sit alone."

I wiped my hand slowly on a napkin as I thought over my reply. I finally wrote back, "I prefer it this way."

"Why?" he wrote back.

"Why does it matter to you?" I angrily typed without thinking. I quickly erased the message and instead sent, "This way I know I am in good company."

"How do you know I am not good company if you haven't even tried to get to know me yet?"

I pondered this. He made a valid point. I was begrudged to agree with him. "Fair point. I still prefer to be alone. I'm not really a people person," I replied.

"You're an only child, aren't you?" he smiled up while his friends were in a heated debate.

I shook my head then typed back, "Not all children without siblings are loners."

"I know that. A fair amount of them seem to be."

"How so?" I looked up quizzically.

He nodded to several tables with single occupants just like mine. I felt my tablet indicate I had a message. I looked down, "Betsy Morgan, single child, single parent family. Brandon is an only child from Quadrant Two. Terrance is also an only child from The City."

"How do you know all these people?" I skeptically looked up after sending my message.

"I talk to people," Thomas simply replied.

I heard the bell gong and I looked up. "Shoot," I muttered.

"Better hurry up or you will be late for class," Thomas got up from his own chair and dumped his scraps in the disposer. He waved to me as he left. I nodded back. I saw a smirk on Kyra's face as we stared at each other. I resisted rolling my eyes and quickly headed to my own class.

Thomas would approach at random times of

the day, initiating conversation despite my attempts to ignore him. On one of these occasions, I swirled around and confronted him, "Are you just unable to take a hint?"

A smile broke across his face, "I knew if I kept talking to you, I would eventually wear you down."

"What is that supposed to mean?" I demanded.

"Well, you're talking to me now, aren't you?" he giggled.

I rolled my eyes and began stomping away from him. With his long legs it didn't take him very long to catch up to me. "Look," he insisted. "I'm not going to give up. That's one of the great things about me."

"What are you expecting of me?" I flopped down on a bench just under one of the trees outside the dorms.

"I only ask for friendship, nothing more."

"Then you are asking for too much," I mumbled.

"No one should be alone," his face clouded over.

I studied his expression. He usually radiated light and kindness. As he said this, I had a sense perhaps I had misjudged him a bit. A nagging feeling tugged on me. I took a slow breath, "We should probably get to know each other a bit more if you insist on pestering me," I suggested.

The cloudy expression disappeared as quickly as it had appeared, "Fantastic!" he grinned.

I shook my head, "You are going to drive me crazy," I sighed.

"Perfect, you know exactly what to expect of me then."

"Sure," I pulled out my tablet from my bag.

A bell gonged in the distance. "I better get going," I looked up to see the sun sinking along the tree line.

"Already?" he looked at his watch. "We are done for the day. Where do you have to go?"

"You're nosey, aren't you?" I silently admired his bluntness.

"I don't mean to be," Thomas bit at his lower lip.

"I have a meeting with Master Kinnet," I finally admitted.

"Isn't she the Master who can't speak?" he looked intently at me.

"Yes," I stood up and brushed some dust off

my pants. "She can't speak. And I can't see well. At least I have something in common with her." I wasn't sure why my anger always boiled to the surface. I felt like I had to always justify myself whenever someone questioned me. I felt the familiar pressure of anxiety welling up in my chest.

"I meant no offense," Thomas looked hurt. I stared at him, trying to determine if he was being genuine or not. I saw the crease at the corners of his eyes and his eyebrows had shot up an inch in sincere concern.

"Look, it's okay. I'm sorry. I shouldn't have been so defensive. I just don't like talking about it."

"Maybe someday you will tell me your story," he pursed his lips.

"To someday then," I tried to smile. I waved to him as I walked away. Thomas was a bit odd and very blunt. I had the feeling he would be the type of person who wouldn't even try to lie even if he could.

Our meeting by the benches became a regular thing in the evenings before I headed to Atheara's. I had learned he had many siblings and was a middle child. I told him about my parents and living in Quadrant 12. After a month or so of our new-found friendship he finally asked me,

"What happened to your eyes, anyway?"

"I love how blunt you are," I sarcastically replied.

"Come on," he rolled his eyes. "Are we going to do this every time I ask you a question?

A group of girls walked by. I heard one of them snicker, whispering my name and pointing at me. I got up to leave but Thomas had a hold of my arm. "Please," he looked at me with pleading eyes.

"Fine," I sighed. I sat back down on the bench, my bag thumping on the grassy ground. He leaned in a bit to hear me. "My eyes got these horrible lines the day my parents took me to The Temple to be admitted into the Seer Guild. They were asking me questions. I tried to use the fatras. The next thing I knew I was in the infirmary and couldn't see. The doctors didn't think I would be able to see again. Eventually I was able to sort of see."

"Sort of?" Thomas looked intrigued.

"I can see the fatras lines all the time. It's like a switch was flipped and now I can't turn it off," admitting this to him was like pulling out a poisonous truth from my body. "That's why I go to Atheara. She is trying to help me see beyond the lines. They don't think I will ever fully recover my normal sight. She is training me to be able to handle it."

"Did you ever consider just not training at all and going home? That's what the other kids were saying when you started joining our classes."

"I tried. Every time I tried, I got really bad headaches. I had to give up trying to ignore the Seer 'gifts'," I put up my hands for air quotes.

"I'm glad you didn't give up," Thomas leaned back.

"Why?" I looked at him.

"Then I wouldn't have the pleasure of annoying you every day," he laughed.

"Nice," I stood up again. "I better get going. Atheara will be upset with me if I am late."

"Okay," Thomas stood up too. "However, I was being honest when I said I was glad you didn't quit. I'm glad Master Kinnet is able to help you."

I stared at him for a moment, tilting my head to the side trying to decide if he was being truly sincere. I decided to take him at his word and nodded. As I walked across the grass to Atheara's residence I wondered if Thomas was truly trying to be my friend. Or if he was just being nice so he could get the real story about the crazy girl with golden lines through her eyes.

Three times a year we were allowed to visit

our families back home. Some of the students stayed at the Centre during these times due to unexpected plan changes. Most of the time I went home to be in the secluded comfort of my parents. They kept my room the same way I had left it. We sat around the plain, silver table eating dinner. Mother was a culinary genius, probably due to her capabilities in botany.

"Pandria, you would never have guessed!" Father exclaimed over a mouthful of an elegant baked chicken salad. "I have been promoted. Stal-Tech has become one of the largest engineering companies."

"That's great Father," I smiled up at him. I saw a tendril of a golden line snake away from him. Mentally I pulled at the string. I could see the opulent sparkling future he might have at Stal-tech. I looked back up to him and gave him a big grin. He smiled back and nodded, returning to his food.

"You know, Pandria, we have enough money to go shopping tomorrow. We can maybe find a nice dress to match the sparkling gold in your eyes," she looked at me hopefully. I knew she was trying to set up a fun day out together. The reminder made me grimace a bit. My green eyes had faded to gray. They still had the spidery webs other Seers had, mine were a golden thread rather than a pale color the other potentials had in their eyes.

I swallowed the bitterness which tried to creep up every time I recalled my near blind experience. I forced a smile for her. I didn't know if she saw the anger roll across my face as she was smiling when I looked up; both of us put on a brave face. The Seers had warned me. I had my vision back. Yet, the episode may happen again at any given time. I tried hard not to fear the possibility. I constantly watched my own tendrils of fatras snake out; looking for warning signs I was heading down a path which might permanently erase my sight. The rest of dinner was a familiar, comfortable silence for us. Afterwards, I sat with Mother in the herb garden tending to the hybrids she had been trying to grow. When the sun fully vanished, I went inside and cleaned my dirty hands, washing away the warmth of the soil. As I lay in bed, I could see the stars stark white against the ink bruised sky wondering what it would be like to be amongst the stars and look down upon the world.

The next morning showed only a dull brightness. My Mother still held onto the enthusiasm she tried to inject into me last night. We quickly got dressed and grabbed our umbrellas just in case the skies opened up and began to pour down on us. The markets were lined against a small lake waterfront. In times long gone things were mass produced. These days things were hand-crafted. The machines of old were long torn apart. We were no longer over consuming our land.

Betsy's shop was a small cottage filled to the rafters with hats, skirts, blouses, and other clothing. I could smell the linen and felt each thread of the hand sewn flowers and decorations on the varying skirts. Betsy was certainly a skilled seamstress.

"Good day, ladies," Betsy's elderly voice called from the back of the shop. "Will I be!" she exclaimed when she saw me. "Pandria my dear I didn't know you were going to be home," she smiled warmly at me. "Come child, I have just a thing for a person with your talents." Most people reacted this way to Seers. One of the things the advisors ingrained into our training. We are the symbols of hope and prosperity. In return, we must act the role.

"Thank you," I followed her.

The dress was made of the finest silk I had ever seen. Gold thread was carefully woven into flowers and elegant curves. The silk itself was an ivory color.

"This is beautiful," Mother fingered the dress with awe. "Though I am unsure we can afford such fine quality," she wistfully sighed.

"For Pandria, I ask for only a fifth of its price."

"We couldn't," Mother began.

I looked at her with concern. Offending Betsy was not on my list of things to do for today. I reflected back on the lectures from Master Reese on Leadership and recalled the best thing to do in a situation like this was to seem gracious while trying to raise the price a bit. I didn't want to feel like we were taking advantage of people. I wondered if Kyra had such objections to such enormous generosity. It probably didn't faze her growing up in the city and having wealth. "You are gracious Betsy. Let us at least pay ten percent for the fine craftsmanship."

"You are as generous as you are gifted, Pandria," the old woman smiled at me.

With the price being settled we paid for the dress and went for a walk around the other stores. Mother chatted about the other girls in the neighborhood. Most of my peers had already turned twelve. My birthday was in a week. I had just enough time at home to celebrate and then head back to the Centre.

"Mother?" I looked over at her as I licked at the edge of my ice cream cone. "Have you heard from Marisol?"

"I saw them the other week. Hasn't she written to you since you left?"

I shook my head no and averted my eyes away from her. My heart tugged and I tried to drown the feeling out through another bite of ice cream.

"Marisol may be getting ready to choose her own path right now, taking tests to see where her aptitude is," Mother rested a reassuring hand on my shoulder.

I closed my eyes and tried to construct Marisol's face in my mind. I let it fill my thoughts and then transferred the feeling of friendship I had with her into a track edging away from me. We had just begun to learn how to do this in our practicum class. I finally found her in a playground sitting alone. Her foot scuffed at the dirt on the ground as she was staring at another group of girls. I pulled my thoughts back to Mother and my ice cream.

"You see her?" Mother inquired, a puzzled expression on her face.

I nodded.

"What is it like?" Mother asked. "Are you able to see from a distance?"

I knew Mother well enough to know she didn't ask out of just awe and fascination. She was genuinely curious about my gift. The Masters had told us non-Seers would be curious about our talents. Some would even try to take advantage of those talents. We were to be vigilant. In this case, it was Mother. I wasn't too worried.

"I have to concentrate really hard. They say it's because we are just learning how to use our talents. They say it gets easier with practice. Sometimes, when I look, I see lines darting away from me. When I want to look for someone specifically, I have to bring their image in my mind. I have to stretch that image and focus on a feeling I have of the person. I look around with my mind, trying to see an illuminated line. Once I find a line brighter than the rest, I follow it until I come across the person I am looking for." I finished.

"Sounds hard," Mother sounded impressed. I smiled at her. The feeling of the facial muscles pulling up into a smile felt foreign to me. I realized I had better make the best of what I have otherwise smiling would always feel abnormal to me.

The week slipped by in a haze. As usual, my time with my parents felt short. My parents honored my request for a simple birthday, just the three of us. I had no siblings, just my parents and me. Life was quiet for us until I started showing signs of the Seers. After I left, my parents remained in a modest lifestyle. Our community was a close net community on Southwest Quadrant of the 3rd Circle from Kastor, The City. Small communities circled the big city. The Communities became more condensed the closer you were to the big city and the Centre. They were circles upon circles of communities until you reached The City, Centre, and Temple. There were many more circles after our own circle before you reached the Outer Ridge and the Barrens. Our life was built as a defense from Barren raiders who still held onto the barbaric way of life. In time, they stopped attacking our civilization. All was quiet and peaceful.

The train ride back to the Centre was a long one. My Father rode with me though I was now old enough to make it back on my own. We hadn't had much Father and daughter time.

The set-up for the train was like spokes of a wheel; the outer Communities has a line leading directly back to the Centre and big city, Kastor. The Communities were set up so nature was prevalent and could be seen everywhere. Some felt we needed to emphasize nature's beauty since the Barrens were devoid of such things.

Father and I spoke about the wonderful sites we saw as we passed by. I had to concentrate to look past the interlacing lines arcing all over the place. The train pulled into the depot just inside the Centre. Beautiful orchids grew between aspen trees which blew lightly with the breeze of spring. He helped me carry my bag to my bed and hugged me tightly.

As I lay in bed later in the night, the moon's light stretched across my face. I stared through the window, watching the light refract in soft hued colours. Seeing the colours beyond the golden threads was difficult; seeing them was worth it.

CHAPTER 2:
THE CENTRE

Atheara had implemented a new, rigorous training session with her at least once a week on top of my other classes. I would attend these sessions in the evening before I went to dinner. She was teaching me how to deal with my handicap. The Masters had agreed she would be best suited to help me reach beyond my impairment. Seeing fatras lines all the time complicated my training as I often lost focus, a skill imperative to becoming a functional Seer.

The light swirled around, golden threads flowing out before me. I reached out to touch the threads, fingers caressing the air. I looked over my shoulder and saw a fiery line stretch behind me. To the side I saw a grey tinged line drawn out into a murky fog. Many other lines darted out as I slowly lost my focus. The lights of the multitude of fatras started searing my sight, my eyes watering as I fought against the blindness. I shifted slightly from sitting cross-legged in the

Arboretum. Atheara had left me some time ago so she could rest. I struggled with my ailment, suffering from the searing hot pain every time I looked upon the fatras. The pain had been blinding for the first couple weeks of recovery. I fidgeted, wistfully sighing at the sound of laughter from the sunny outside teasing me. I had no urge to go outside, though, and see the infinite amount of fate lines emanating from my fellow students. Atheara had put faith in me, taking me under her wing, teaching me how to control my sight.

I absentmindedly drew circles in the dirt I was sitting on. I was having trouble focusing to attune my sight to see the fatras. The desire to do so was simply not in me. I let go of my fatras and imagined a cool, clear bubble. This was something Atheara had taught me when the fatras became too unbearable. I didn't want to leave to go home and abandon my training now I was beginning to feel some sort of normalcy here. Nor did I have the desire to stay here while the other students stared at me like I was an aberration of some kind. I simply wanted to continue studies in horticulture. I wanted to follow in Mother's career path. However, I quickly learned avoiding the fatras was not an option. I had tried for the first full week after I woke up from the episode to ignore the fatras. I tried to deny my own powers. In the end I settled for trying to control the new ailment so I could get rid of the headaches which pounded against my temples every time I tried to ignore the fatras. They were always in my line of vision.

I sighed and closed my eyes letting the clear bubble dissipate. As I slowly reopened my eyes, I concentrated on the fatras, noticing how they pulsed away from me. I then pulled back my sight and tried to focus on the details of the plants; the dew drop sliding down the petal of the carnation leaf, the pollen from the stamen of the sunflowers, the earthen soil permeating the greenhouse. I could see these details finally.

"Very good Pandria. You are starting to become at ease with your new vision," I heard Atheara's voice inside my head.

Beads of sweat tickled my forehead and I brushed them away with the back of my dusty hand, leaving smudges of dirt across my face. I heard Atheara's tinkle laughter. "It's just dirt," I mumbled.

She handed me a towel. I scrubbed off the dirt from my face. Wordlessly Atheara motioned me to follow her. We walked into her common room, the lights dimmed, the setting sun throwing golden light throughout the room. I looked around, wondering what it would be like to see a normal sunset again without all the lines crisscrossing through my vision.

"You will see the sun set again, Little One," Atheara brushed away a curl creeping up behind my ear. I flinched at the touch. The only people I had ever really felt close to were my own parents. Atheara pretended to not take notice and hugged me gently.

"You are not alone," her voice washed over me. I relaxed a bit and hugged her back. For the first time since coming here I actually believed perhaps I was not alone.

Days slid by one after another and soon, a rhythmic pattern took over my life. I woke in the mornings to study the regular Academics other children my age were studying: sciences, math, technology, reading, and writing. My afternoons were dominated by Seer Training. I still found it hard to focus on the everyday activities. In the evenings with Atheara, I found some rest in the hectic blur of classes. Three years passed in this steady pattern. I studied, trained, and visited my family whenever possible.

"Pandria, would you please stay focused," Master Barnsworth sighed.

"Sorry Ma'am," I replied. I had become distracted following a tendril of golden thread down a possible future. I had been gazing at it while Master Barnsworth rambled on about the history of the first Seer, Erik. His story wasn't boring. I had just heard it multiple times before. The tendril I was following meandered out from the floor. I let my mind focus more on it than the story Master Barnsworth was relating to us.

"Come to me child after your lesson," Atheara's voice whispered inside my mind. She had insisted on using her first name while all the Masters went by the traditional usage of their last names.

"Is everything all right?" I thought back to her. Only silence followed. I would have been frustrated had this not been a normal occurrence between us. Atheara had taken an interest in me. During our times together she would say very little which suited me just fine. I wasn't much into friendships and trust wasn't something I was too keen to share. Thomas and I had developed a sort of friendship. Thomas was more interested in sports than philosophizing during free time; not that we had much free time.

"Your assignment for this week is to write an essay on the basics of Seer abilities and how they are associated with the original Seer," Master Barnsworth concluded. I breathed inward and counted to ten to prevent myself from audibly sighing. This was something my advisor insisted upon since many of the Masters were complaining about my lack of interest in their classes. At least this way they couldn't audibly hear my distraught about the assignments they gave us.

I was able to do the work and I wasn't lazy. The work just bored me. Thomas encouraged me through every class. Even his enthusiasm started to wear thin on me. His growing friendship with Kyra exacerbated the issue. Thomas and I were simply friends, nothing more. If only Kyra would see this, we would all get along. In my presence she became more intimate with Thomas. She seemed to focus on making sure I knew my relationship with him was nothing more than camaraderie.

Traversing across The Centre's grounds had become second nature to me. The Centre was separated by four parts. In the middle of the circle was The Temple. Walking through the flower plaza on my way to The Master's quarters I passed by a gaggle of girls who were sifting through pamphlets of the newest dress styles. I passed some of the more refined students who relished in the lavish possessions which our society tried to force upon the more fortunate. This felt wrong to me. I bit back a retort and passed them without comment. Offending them would prove fruitless. I found Atheara meditating in the comfort of her solar room where exotic plants of all shapes and colors surrounded her.

"Good afternoon, Pandria. Please sit and I will be with you in a moment," her voice whispered in my head. She held a talent of being able to multitask, speaking to you with her mind while searching down a fragile fatras string. I often found her like this and had learned to wait patiently.

I sat my bag down, sitting cross legged near her. I inhaled the rich soil smell which filled the Solar Room. I practiced focusing on the small details of the dirt. Having the vision etched into my retinas made it difficult to see anything past the line of fatras which tangled throughout our world. Atheara, the therapists, and advisors had worked with me constantly to look past these lines so I may be able to see the world as it is instead of seeing just the fatras.

"You are getting better at focusing, Little One," her voice held a hint of humor.

Atheara was the only one I allowed to call me little. She was well into her 50's. Her age and wisdom brought a sense of respect from me. A respect not often earned from others.

"You called," I sarcastically replied.

A smile tugged at the corner of her wrinkled cheeks. "Mind your manners Little One or I will increase your workload."

This was the same threat Atheara always used; a sort of joke between the two of us. I laughed. Something I usually only did around the elderly woman.

"I have been studying the lines carefully and there is something that disturbs me," she began. I knew better than to interrupt once she started. "There are just as many fatras as usual. Yet, they all disappear when you follow them outward."

"Wait, what?" I asked her.

"They disappear," she patiently repeated.

"How is that possible?" I asked.

"I am unsure, Pandria."

"Why are you not telling the Great Seers?" I jumped to my feet.

"Sit Little One," she commanded.

"But,"

"Listen to me."

I slowly sat back down. "If I thought they would have more answers than I do, I would have gone to them. I believe they do not. They have not seen this as I have which makes me wonder what is truly happening here. Would not the Great Seers have seen such a thing already? Would they not be speaking to the Masters about such a thing?" Atheara stated.

I sat back on my heels. I let my thoughts flow and let go of the images before my eyes, embracing the sight of the gilded threads. I followed them down. I started to think Atheara had seen wrong when I found the abrupt edge of the fatras. Just beyond the edge of society there was a break in the threads. I gasped and was brought back to the Solar Room.

"Atheara," I cried. "What was that? The lines don't just disappear, they are cut off."

"You see it too," Atheara stated.

"Yes," I stated. "I would have missed it if you hadn't encouraged me to look further. I might not have seen it otherwise. What are we going to do?"

"I'm not sure," Atheara said. "I will have to speak to the Masters about this. I want you to keep an eye on this situation."

"Why me?"

"Why not you?" a smile ghosted across Atheara's face.

Atheara remained quiet which always indicated she was done with me. I quietly rose and slung my carrier bag over my shoulder, books thumping against my thigh. I inhaled the sweet scents of the fauna mixed with the richness of the soil again and exited the heated room. The cool breeze took me by surprise. I could feel my cheeks flush. I glanced back at Atheara wondering why she had brought me here to see the ending of the fatras.

As I was crossing the complex, "Catching you sneaking off with a boy?" Thomas' laughter cracked through the evening air.

"Of course not," I scowled and stalked past him.

"Good evening to you, too, Pandria," he stepped in line with me.

"Where's your girlfriend?" I hissed back.

"Never you mind," he slid his gaze to me briefly.

I opened the oaken doors which lead to the cafeteria of the Centre. Smells of roast fought against the smells of baked salmon. They always tried to offer as much variety as possible; many of us had come from varying regions.

"Speak of evil and they shall appear," I muttered.

"What was that dear?" Kyra grabbed Thomas' hand.

"I said it's lovely to see you," I smiled and charged to the food line.

"Must be hungry," Thomas suppressed a grimace. He always tried to smooth the peace between us. He usually let me have my space when Kyra was around. He seemed very keen to not give up this time.

"What did the grand, old Atheara want?" Thomas casually asked.

"The same as usual: be a good girl, pay attention in class, blah, blah, blah," I answered. I wasn't going to share close secrets with Kyra around. I never knew who else would know what I said by the time I went to bed. Not that I ever caught her at it.

I placed my finger upon the scanner which automatically deducted from a food fund the Seers set up for every potential. When we were eventually interned out in the field, we would work off what we would owe for food and housing. They calculated a running tally and never charged us much since we were considered valuable.

I thought Kyra and Thomas would go hunker down in their usually two-person spot, but Thomas followed me to an open table. Ignoring this I asked him, "So, how was your day?"

As per her usual, Kyra answered for him, "It was great!" She proclaimed. "We wandered the gardens during the noon break, and I got top marks in our practicum."

I fought not to raise my eyebrows as I responded, "That's great."

Thomas looked as if he were biting back a laugh. "And what about you, Pandria? How was your day?"

"I heard you fell asleep in history again," Kyra supplied for me.

"I didn't fall asleep," my defenses rose up. "I was working on controlling the fatras."

Before Kyra could respond Thomas interjected, "Well I'm ready for another break. They are really loading us up with the work lately," Thomas tried to veer the conversation back to a neutral ground. Being a child of four must have its advantages. He seemed to know how to steer the conversation away from dangerous ground.

Kyra tossed her long black hair over her shoulder, "Well, I think Father is going to take me to see the Central Library the next break we have."

"Because we don't see enough books here?" sarcasm dripped from my voice.

"You know Pandria, never one to pour over old

books," Thomas tried to turn it into a joke.

I gave him one of my winning smiles and quickly gulped down the rest of my salad. "I better get going. I have to write the essay for history," I got up without looking back. I could feel Thomas' eyes on me. I didn't dare look back. I dumped my tray at the kitchen collection counter and headed to the study hall.

The vaulted ceiling rose high above, made of the same crystal all the other windows were made of. During the night, the star's light mutely refracted throughout the big hall. Tables with plush chairs were arranged in an orderly manner with dividers between the single tables at the very end of the hall to allow for some privacy. I pulled out my tablet and began typing my essay for class. I knew the history so well by this point I had no need to bring out my history book. I was just finishing the last paragraph when I heard Thomas' voice in the next table on the other side of my divider.

"What was that all about, really?" he asked through the divider.

"I can only assume you are speaking to me?" I peered around the divider.

"No, I thought I would talk to my alter ego?" He sarcastically retorted. He pulled his chair around the divider.

"Where's your better half?" I went back to my essay.

"Homework."

"And this is something you are avoiding?" I glanced over and saw no papers or books.

"Thought I would get the real reason why Atheara wanted to see you," Thomas responded. This was one of the things which made him my friend besides his awful sarcasm. He was able to get straight to the point.

"Have you tried to follow the fatras past the last circle of Communities?" I asked.

"Um, no, why?" he scrunched up his eyebrows.

"Atheara showed me today. They just cut off. They are disappearing."

"Disappearing? Are you sure?"

Another wonderful thing about Thomas; he knew when to cut the sarcasm and take me seriously. "I saw it myself."

I saw him shut his eyes. Some potentials saw the lines of the fatras with their mind's eye rather than looking out at them like I did. "I see them just fine," he finally responded.

"What do you mean they are fine?" I stared at him incredulously.

"Meaning I don't see them cut off. Maybe you just misread what you saw," he tried to patronize me.

"Are you serious, Thomas?" I whispered. "I know what I saw." I took in a deep breath, counted to ten, and then let my gaze focus on the fatras. Thomas had been my friend long enough to know when I was looking at the fatras. My gaze took me past the study hall and out into the night. The string vibrated as I followed it down past the Centre and out into The Communities. I reached the edge as I did last time and stopped short of the Barrens. The lines disappeared into nothingness again. I quickly inhaled as I was abruptly brought back. Thomas must have seen something in my gaze because he was grabbing my shoulder and shaking me.

"Pandria are you alright?" he exclaimed. The other students who were studying were now focusing on the two of us. The Master of the Word came over.

"Is everything all right here, Thomas?" his kindly voice inquired.

"Yes Master, sorry," Thomas apologized.

The Master of Words was not ready to accept this. "She's shaking and white. Child, I think we need to get you to the Infirmary," he placed a gentle hand on my other shoulder.

I looked up at Thomas with a scared look. He understood me without any words. I had once explained to him how my eyes took on the golden lines and my long days in the Infirmary in darkness. He knew I did whatever I needed to so I could avoid the hospital.

"Master, if I may take her to Atheara I think she could help in this matter," he tried to get me to my feet. I swayed and fell, feeling Thomas' warm hands and the Master of Words catch me before I hit the floor.

I woke up with sunlight shining brightly through a window next me. Atheara was resting in the chair next to the bed I was lying in. I carefully lifted the covers and hunted for my clothes. The nurses probably took the clothes off me when I was admitted into the Infirmary.

The Infirmary was not my most favorite place in the Centre. The nurses had no sense of humor or bedside manner. Bad memories still haunted this place for me. The walls were a bare color and the windows were a plain cut glass. The only way I could describe the floors was simply sterile. The place smelled of sickly sweetness. I was once told it was to help ailing patients recover. All it seemed to do for me was make me nauseous.

"Running away so soon, Little One?"

"Do you see me running Atheara?" I said. She

could hear and in public I chose to use my voice rather than try to speak to her with my mind.

"A figure of speech as you well know," she reprimanded. "And where do you think you are going?"

"Somewhere not here," I countered.

"Sit," She commanded. She didn't often command me. I knew she was serious.

I sat down and pulled my socks on. "I don't like it here."

"Nor do I but you need to rest and recover," she patted my hand.

"Recover from what, exactly?" I asked. "I feel fine."

She pulled a mirror out from a nearby table and handed it to me. I gave her a quizzical look and pulled it up to my face. Golden lines were starting to etch around my cheek bones and my face was almost pure white. I gasped.

"Yes, Little One, you have certainly done it now," Atheara chided.

"What's happened?" I almost screamed.

"Hush child or they will kick me out," Atheara reprimanded.

I bit my lip which threatened to quiver as tears

rolled down my face.

"Breathe, Pandria," her voice whispered in my ear. She began to hum the tune my Mother used to hum to me when I was younger. My breathing took on the cadence of the song. The shaking slowed to a stop.

"Thank you, Atheara," I whispered.

She hugged me tightly. "What were you doing before this happened?"

I swallowed hard knowing I hadn't kept my promise of keeping her secret to myself. "I told Thomas about the fatras cutting off. He said he didn't see it. I looked for myself again and then, nothing," I lamely finished.

"Nothing?" Her eyebrows arched.

"I passed out or something," I said. "There was just blackness."

"Pandria, listen to me carefully. I don't want you to look again until we better understand this. Do you hear me?"

"Yes, yes."

She pulled at my chin and forced me to look into her eyes, "Promise me."

"I, I promise Atheara."

"Do I tell the Great Seers what I saw?" I looked

down at the floor, ashamed at not keeping the information to myself.

"Do not feel you betrayed me, Pandria," her voice took on a kinder tone than usual. "I have already spoken to the Great Seers. They are aware of what you and I both saw. They also have been in to check on you."

I audibly sighed, frustrated at the attention. Atheara held back a smirk.

CHAPTER 3: INFIRMARY

Thomas came to check on me while I was in the Infirmary. He didn't bring Kyra along for which I was grateful. I was already frustrated at being kept in the Infirmary. I didn't need her cynical words towards me as well.

"And how are we feeling today?" Thomas cheerfully asked.

"You have someone in your pocket?" I smirked.

"Okay then, how are you feeling?" a look of concern crossed his face. I hadn't looked into the mirror. I avoided my reflection whenever possible. I must still look like a wreck.

"That bad? I won't get many dates this way," I tried to brush it off.

"Naw, I think the golden line look matches your eyes," he bantered back.

"Nice," I shook my head.

He dumped a pile of homework on one of the chairs near my bed. "Out of all the things you could have brought me you bring me homework?" I grumped.

"Well, they wouldn't let me bring in the cookies you love from the cafeteria, so I had to improvise."

"You are just chalk full of fun today," I flipped through a diagram of fatras.

Thomas slumped onto the empty chair by my bed. "When are they releasing the prisoner?" he inquired.

"Great question," I said.

"She will be released in a couple more days," Nurse Franine stated.

"See, only a couple more days," he punched my arm.

"Yes, just in time for break," I slapped the books beside my bed. They threatened to topple over. "Too bad I will be spending it catching up."

"You aren't going home?"

"I am going home. I will need to take all this with me. I know we are only gone a week, but I need to make sure I don't get behind." I was bored with the lessons they were teaching. I still felt the need to keep decent grades for the sake of my parents. I didn't want to disappoint them. "They have been in contact with my parents and apprised them of my 'condition'," I made air quotes with my fingers. "I'm surprised Mother didn't come busting the door down."

"I think Nurse No Fun had something to do with that," Thomas whispered. I looked over and saw her attending a Potential who seemed to have a broken arm. We were required to partake in physical activities besides our studies. For some of us who were non-athletic this proved to be dangerous.

"And what are you and your one true love doing?" I asked.

"She is going home to her family. I am off to my Uncle's."

"Family get together?" I tried not to laugh.

"Of course," he smiled.

A gong sounded in the distance and Thomas stretched. "Guess I better run off to Study Hall. Wouldn't want to have to study during the break," he laughed.

"Ha, ha," I grumbled again as he headed out the door.

I slid under the covers and closed my eyes.

The morning light was ashen; the spring storms had finally arrived. Father was at the train depot waiting for me. I lugged my bag over my shoulder and rolled the other bag which held my clothes. I could hear him suck in a quick breath. He didn't say anything when I stopped in front of him. He threw his arm around me and pulled the bag off my shoulder.

"Let's go," he smiled. We found a seat at the back of the train and watched in silence as we rolled away from the Centre. The silence was as companionable as it once was before I became a Seer. I could feel his eyes glance at me from time to time. Concern wrinkled his eyes.

I looked down the train, the other seats were filled with other students heading home for the break. Many got off at the first stop, the city of Kastor. I felt a lump in my throat as several of the pristine girls openly stared at me. They nudged each other off the train. I bit down on my lip, refusing to let the tears burning the back of my eyelids pour forth. The lights of the fatras began to swirl around me, coalescing into a mess of stark whites, golds, reds, and consuming blacks. My head throbbed as each thread pounded upon my eyes, causing the already burning sensation to grow.

I closed my eyes and recalled Atheara's voice, "Breathe in, breathe out. In the rhythm of a slow beat march. With each step a pure, white bubble envelops you, wrapping your senses in a blanket of calm, soothing flow protecting you from the fatras."

The last word echoed in my mind as the bubble appeared. The racing fatras faded and I was back in control. I slowly opened up my eyes. My Dad's face was turned away from me. I could see him looking at me from the corner of his eye. He quickly looked away when he noticed I was looking back. I bit my lip and stared out the window, hoping the scenery would distract me from my distress.

I was happy to rush off the train and take the rail to our home. The smell of honeysuckle invaded my senses. I inhaled deeply, home.

Mother was singing in the kitchen. I could hear the crackling of something frying.

"Smells good," I put on a smile.

She looked at me and bit her lip. I could see her shoulders tense; then threw her arms around me. I could smell the lavender soap she used every day.

"Don't smother her, darling," Father gently pulled her off of me. I could feel the moisture of tears on my shirt. Ignoring this, I picked up my bags, and headed to my room. I dumped them on the floor by my bed. Flopping on my faded comforter I stared up at the woody ceiling. Taking in deep breaths I slowed my racing heart. I knew they would react to my physical change. I wasn't prepared for how upset they would be.

I rolled back up and stared at my bags. Pulling out the books Thomas had brought me I began sifting through the list of homework I needed to do. I knew I could do it in one night. I thought spacing it out would give me a good excuse to be alone whenever I felt awkward around my parents.

"Knock, knock," Father peaked through the door. "I see you are settling in."

"Thomas was kind enough to bring me my homework while I was in the Infirmary," I held up the stack of books.

"How is Thomas doing?" Father sat at the edge of my bed.

My parents had met Thomas a couple of times when they were allowed to come visit. They were interested to know about one of the few friends I had at the Centre. They found him funny and entertaining; vastly different from some of the other stuffier potentials.

"He's good. Kyra keeps him hopping," I rolled my eyes.

"I don't sense jealousy, do I?" Father eyed me

critically.

"No, no. We're just friends. She's just pushy," I corrected him.

"Well, maybe you should try to become friends with her."

"And what exactly do we have in common?"

"Thomas," Father patted my knee.

"Yea, yea."

"Dinner!" Mother called from the kitchen.

I started to get up, but Father placed a hand on my shoulder. "Hold on. I know it seems awkward being home after what happened. Just know we love you and are concerned."

"I know Dad. I just don't know how to feel."

"You don't have to feel any way. We are still family."

I gave him a hug and then jumped off the bed heading to the kitchen. Mother was sitting at the table already. We sat down, the tension in the air settled. Things began to feel normal. The air was lighter, and we felt more like a family again. Mother chatted about a cross breed of lavender she had created from honeysuckle.

"We are still testing the stability of the plant. I think it would be interesting to use the combo in a salad."

I went to bed early. I was perpetually tired since my new episode. The doctors were unsure how long this side effect would last.

The darkness of sleep claimed me immediately. I was plagued with dreams like when I was a very young child. Everything ended in an abrupt and painful coldness. Everywhere I tried to walk in my dream pain followed me. Buildings from my childhood crumbled to dust. I was alone, the sun shone brightly through a dusty haze.

Each morning I woke up I saw dark circles under my eyes. The bright shine of the gold lines around my cheeks reflected back at me. I tried to scrub both away with the palm of my hand. Nothing helped. I spent time with Mother in the market. At night I would stargaze with Dad; in my sleep the nightmares continued. Towards the end of my stay, I was screaming in my sleep. My parents took turns coming in to check on me, smoothing my sweat plastered hair away from my face. During the day, we were a normal family; the night was another matter entirely.

On the last day my parents looked upon me with unease etched upon their faces. Father rode with me in silence. At my sleeping quarters he hugged me longer than normal.

I was hunkered down in the study hall when Thomas arrived back to the Centre. I had put off my homework due to the lack of sleep. The time had come where I had to finish it. The doctors had cleared me to return to classes. They insisted I had to return to my sleeping quarters by seven every night instead of staying up late like my fellow Potentials to complete all the necessary work. I still had a half hour to go before I had to mandatorily go to bed.

"You don't look so good," Thomas frowned.

"Hello to you too," I said without looking up.

"Not a good visit?" He sat down uninvited.

"No, it was good. Just not sleeping well."

"Homework finally got the best of you," he tried to get a smile from me.

"Of course not," I slammed the book cover down.

"Done?"

"Yup," I stretched.

Thomas scooped up the books and motioned for me to head on out. "You must have heard about my curfew?" I asked him.

"Of course."

"Your girly friend must be back then?"

"Don't start," Thomas uncharacteristically took on a serious tone.

I looked up at him startled to see a frown crease his usually smooth forehead. "Is everything okay?" I nudged his shoulder. Being the same height had its advantages. He struggled to keep the books balanced in his arms.

"Oops, sorry," I giggled.

He started laughing which broke the tension between us. After he calmed down, he stopped and looked at me. "I'm fine, we are okay. I just don't like the fighting between you."

"I know Thomas, I'm sorry. I promise to try to get along with her," I tried to placate him.

"Yea, yea. And the sun will replace the moon someday," he continued on.

We reached the building. Thomas unloaded the books onto the desk beside my bed. "I better get going. See you in the morning?" he inquired.

"Yes, I will be back to classes. Night," I waved at him.

My nightmares still plagued me. I bit back any screams which tried to escape. My fellow Potentials bunked around me probably didn't appreciate this new development. My first night back had been particularly violent.

I was traveling on the train to the Barrens. As I was travelling the tracks disappeared into nothingness. I felt empty and alone. The edges of my vision burned. I felt as if my skin were alite with a thousand fire ants. The pain didn't just consume me physically, it consumed my mental well-being as well. The feeling intensified as I felt a tight pulling sensation in my chest which slowly rose to my throat. This feeling threatened to choke me alive. I waved my hands wildly in front of me, trying to brush the invisible flames away. I felt them sink into my skin, embedding themselves into my flesh. My hands flew to my sides. As the growing pain crawled up to the top of my head, I gave a big heave of breath and sat up in bed. My fingers tightly wound around the pulled-up sheets of the bed. The blankets I had on me when I fell asleep were scattered hopelessly on the floor. Even my pillows had been thrown away from my bed. I could see two very agitated looking roommates glaring at me from my door. My cheeks flared red. I quickly gathered my blankets and pillows, throwing them around me so I couldn't see my door, or my dorm mates, anymore. After two nights of the same dreams, I heard Atheara's voice call out to me.

"Good morning Little One. You have been excused from your morning classes to come see me."

I didn't bother asking her why. My mind was sluggish from the lack of sleep. I could barely focus while in the cafeteria. Breakfast with Thomas and Kyra went by in a foggy haze. I remember dragging my feet to the Solar Room.

"Sit," Atheara ordered.

As soon as I sat, I felt a slow peace fill my mind. The plants and soil here always seem to positively affect me. Maybe that's why Atheara always met me here rather than anywhere else in the Centre.

"I have heard of your night troubles. Tell me about them."

I started at the beginning, seeing my parents and their fears for my well-being. Then I described the emptiness I always came across in my nightmares. I explained to her how everything was crumbling to dust.

"This is disturbing indeed, Young One. You have taken on a much bigger burden than you were meant to carry," she looked straight into my eyes. Something I wasn't used to. Most people gazed at my forehead to avoid looking at the golden lines which flowed through my eyes. "I fear I have put you in danger, having you look into the darkness. You have seen more than you were meant to have seen. For that, I am truly sorry Little One," she looked sad for the first time since I met her. Most of her emotions came across clinical and sarcastic. This new characteristic was foreign to me.

"It wasn't your fault, Atheara," I said. All the sarcasm I usually responded with drained away.

"The Master of the Sleeping Quarters has asked us to move you to a more private location until we can get a handle on this," Atheara bluntly stated.

"Fine," I sighed.

"It's not a punishment, Pandria," she used my real name. This made me look up at her. I realized how sad she truly was.

"What happened while I was gone?" I grasped her wrists. "I hear it in your voice. Not just because I'm not sleeping well or having these crazy nightmares."

"Any great problem is best left for the Great Seers to figure out. You have taken on enough of the burden," Atheara ended the conversation.

She stood up and guided me to my new sleeping quarters which were fairly close to the Solar Room. It was adjoined to Atheara's sleeping quarters. We would share a study area and bathroom. The kitchen and living area were solely for her purposes. I was still to use the cafeteria for eating and the Social Room for visiting with friends. I didn't care too much about the last part as I really only had Thomas.

I knew she was giving up a part of her privacy for me. Maybe to keep me close so she could keep an eye on me. At least I wasn't sent back home. I didn't think I could take Father and Mother's sad looks anymore.

I went to class during the day and at night; Atheara had me drink various herbal remedies to help alleviate some of the nightmares. Two weeks of solid trial and error she finally found a concoction which made me feel groggy at night and refreshed in the morning. I was better to stay with Master Kinnet instead of moving back in with my peers.

A new, steady rhythm began to develop for me. I felt more normal by the day. The golden lines never left my cheek bones. At least I was able to sleep at night. I returned to my studies with my peers. I took the lessons a little more seriously to avoid the gazes the others gave me, the strange girl with the golden lines etched upon her face.

CHAPTER 4:
GREAT COUNCIL
OF SEERS

Three more years had passed by without any more occurrences. I was at the top of the class, surpassing even Kyra. She and Thomas were still dating. I finally found a way to deal with her. I kept her focused on neutral ground as Thomas called it, him. She occasionally showed jealousy towards me whenever I took top scores. For the most part, she kept the edgy quips to herself. I think Thomas may have convinced her smart remarks only hurt their own relationship.

I was applying to an internship outside the Centre. The Great Seers were unsure of how wise this decision would be for me. I had suffered two incidents already. They couldn't find any reason why I needed to stay with the other Potentials any longer. I had already surpassed all the expectations of the Masters and qualified in every subject. I had taken double the classes to speed my education along. I loved staying with Atheara. I didn't have the desire to stay at the Centre any longer than I had to. I was able to look at the fatras without pain as long as I didn't look past The Communities. I still needed to drink the herbal concoction Atheara had created for me to sleep peacefully at night. I was able to perform all Seer duties flawlessly. I had passed the first of the trials.

Each Seer had to pass a trial in order to apply for an internship to prove they were ready to continue on to the next phase of their education. I had filed all the proper paperwork and submitted a lengthy essay on why I felt I was ready, at an early age, to enter into the program. I was given a date and time to meet one of the Masters to go through a series of tests which incorporated history, communication skills, mathematics, literary skills, and practical application of looking at the fatras. This test lasted for five hours making me think they were also testing patience and endurance. Once the scores were tallied, they determined if the scores were sufficient enough to be presented to a panel of Masters and Great Seers in The Temple.

I sat through each of the tests, tapping out the answers onto the terminal testing station I sat at. Master Corinth sat at the back of the classroom so he could see our screens. The terminal was locked to prevent open communication access. We were limited only to the test we were currently taking. Only four others were sitting with me during the test. Every so often I would catch one of the girls sliding a glaring glance at me. With a fleck of her hair, she focused her attention back to her screen. I had become more adept at controlling my anger whenever someone seemed to be judging the marks on my face and eyes. I wasn't about to let them know how much it really bothered me.

I looked back at the fatras theory question I was on. "What was the evolution of the gift of seeing fatras in The Communities?" I tapped on the corner of the keys, thinking carefully about all the aspects affecting the development of our abilities to use the fatras. The only boy in the room huffed. I pulled my hand back away from the keys, giving him an apologetic grin in return. He rolled his eyes and returned to his test. I heard Master Corinth mutter. I couldn't distinguish what he said.

The evolution of the fatras was a complex subject. I knew I wanted to be thorough in my answer. There was the scientific side. Science told us the logical facts. Genetic DNA structures developed certain characteristics which allowed some people to see the fatras. Then there was the historical side of the fatras. I slowly began to develop a structure to my thoughts and began to type. I moved some ideas around as I tried to get a cohesive flow down. A small chime sounded, and we all stopped typing.

"Please exit," Master Corinth's voice echoed in the room. We all got up and went to the hall to take a short break. This continued throughout all of our testing sections. Each section blurring into another.

After it was over, I headed straight to my quarters. I headed into the Arboretum instead of my room. I let the peace of the garden flow through me. Atheara found me sitting quietly like this an hour later.

"Everything okay, Little One?" her steps barely made a sound as she entered.

"Yes, thank you," I stood up and smiled at Atheara.

"Long day?"

"Testing took quite a bit out of me," I admitted.

"That's not like you," Atheara chided.

"What?" I looked at her quizzically.

"Where's your sarcasm?" she laughed.

"It was tested out of me for today," I shrugged.

Later in the night, I tossed and turned. I wanted to know the results from our testing. I wouldn't know if they were acceptable or not until I received a notice. The notice would let me know if I was to meet the panel of Masters and Great Seers or not.

The internship would assist me in passing the second of the trials. The overall success or failure would be the determining factor if I was ready to become an active Seer. The last of the trials would be the final test. There would be a written test and a short-term work portfolio collected during a six-month internship.

A week after the testing I received a message from Master Corinth. "You will see the panel of Masters and Great Seers in a week's time. Any inquiries can be directed to your advisor."

I sighed deeply. In fact, when I saw Kyra, I didn't try to hide away from her like I usually did when Thomas wasn't around. I waved at her with a bit of a smirk. After looking over her shoulder she confusedly waved back and then hurried over to a group of girls at a table at the other corner of the cafeteria. I didn't care. I was happy I might get away from these city girls.

I was dressed in a simple gray dress with a matching jacket. My face still held the marks of my years here. Atheara could enter a room with no noise. However, I still sensed her presence behind me.

"For you," she offered a steel jewel pendant. She gently placed it in my hands, and I fingered its smooth surface.

"Thank you," I said with my mind.

She picked the pendant up out of my hand and placed it around my neck. I hadn't expected the pendant to feel warm. A heat radiated from the jewel.

"Seer's Fortune," Atheara smiled at me.

I had heard of the stone in our studies. There was a rare stone found near the now crumbling ruins amongst the Outer Ridges. Here is where the first Seer, only known by his first name Erik, was said to have lived before our world crumbled to the radiation. To become a Seer was to have a rare fortune for both the one who showed the talent and for the family whom they came from. However, a Seer's Fortune was also named for this precious stone. The Science Guild even believed this rare stone is the very reason why some members of The Communities were able to hold such a valuable gift.

"It is a gift," Atheara read my mind.

"It's beautiful," I tried to smile at her.

She rested her wrinkled hand upon my shoulder. "It is a reminder, Pandria, of who you are and the capabilities I know you have."

I gave her a hug and then brushed at my long hair with the tips of my fingers. I nodded to Atheara. We headed to the Seer Temple.

My shoes whispered against the metal floor. I waited just outside the circle and Atheara went in ahead of me. Atheara once told me she was only a Master because of her ailment. The Great Seer Council still valued her talents. She was allowed a seat in the Council even though she was not considered one of the Great Elder Seers.

My name was called out just a few minutes later and I entered. I inhaled deeply, recalling the first time I had ever been in here. The memories sent chills through me. I pushed away the thoughts and focused on the ring of Great Seers. Atheara was back in her place to the left of me where I first met her. She smiled encouragingly at me.

"We have received your request to intern outside the Centre. There are many of us who are concerned with this choice. Where do you see the fatras taking you?"

"Outside the Centre, Great Seer," I looked up at him. I focused on his forehead where wisps of red hair lay. I didn't want to look into those eyes again and have another episode. Not when I was so close to leaving the Centre.

"And does this fatras mean ill or good for you?" He persisted.

"I admit the line does not prove completely clear, Great Seer. However, it does seem to prove to be a good line to follow."

"She is gifted, Great Council of Seers. I have worked with Pandria for many years now. Her skills have grown considerably. She has suffered, yes. The fatras have not been kind to her. She is beyond the teachings of the Potential, Masters. She can learn nothing more from us here," Atheara spoke to the minds of everyone in the room.

I was touched by her commitment to help me through this. I hadn't realized how much faith she had in me. I didn't know if I was really deserving of such faith. If it came from Atheara, then it was truly what she believed.

"Step into the hall, Pandria. We must discuss this a little further. We will be with you shortly with our answer."

I bowed to the Great Seer and exited the room. I was glad to be out of there. I rubbed at my arms, trying to dispel the chill I felt. I focused on the lines before me. Out the door the line was iridescent. Back through the door to the Great Seer Temple, and where the Council sat, the fatras blazed red. I tried not to let this scare me. Atheara had once told me Seers may often misinterpret what we see. I was hoping this proved true in my case.

"Pandria," I was called back in.

I entered and saw a look of resignation upon the red-haired man's face. "Your internship has been accepted. Peace," he concluded.

I bowed to the Council and exited. Before I could get to the outer door the red-haired man was behind me, pulling at my arm. "Be wary, young Pandria. I fear for you and for our kind. Remember to do what is best for everyone."

Atheara came up behind him and tapped him on the shoulder. "We need to let her get her things and pack. We don't want her to miss the train." She eyed him critically.

"Yes, yes of course. I was just sharing my concerns," he muttered. He rushed off back into the Temple.

I smiled at Atheara. We headed back to our shared home. I rummaged through the closet to find my bags and placed my clothes in them. I would be leaving tomorrow evening and needed to make sure I had everything before leaving. Since my interview was the last one scheduled I knew I might leave in haste. I didn't care too much about hastily leaving. I knew I would miss both Atheara and Thomas. I didn't forge a bond outside of those two people at The Centre.

Atheara knocked on my door. I waved her in while sorting through the books at my bedside. "He is not wrong, Little One."

I looked up at Atheara and noticed tears rolling down her face. "What is it?" I stopped what I was doing. I placed a hand on her arm.

"I see danger in your path, Pandria. With most Potentials I usually have a mentor/student relationship with them. With you. . ."

I gave her a big hug, holding her close. Although I loved my own parents Atheara had filled a place in my heart here at the Centre. Her friendship was going to be one of the few things I would remember with fondness.

We stood there for several minutes. She brushed a tear away from her face. She left my room. I was alone. Fear crept into my heart for the first time since I applied for the internship.

My bags were packed and piled near the door. I didn't have many possessions. Other than the traditional clothing of the Potentials I had maybe one or two dresses my Mother and I bought at the market. The rest of my possessions were my tablet, books, and a few keepsakes. I fingered the necklace Atheara gave me.

I glanced around the room and then headed

out. "Don't be out too late Little One!" I could hear the sing song call of Atheara.

I knew I would find Thomas at the sports court. He usually played a little basketball this time of night. His friends were not on the court with him. There was no sign of Kyra.

"Hey stranger," I waved.

He caught the ball as it bounced towards him. He wiped his hands on his pants. He slowly walked over and nodded.

"Something I said?"

He shook his head and sat down on one of the benches.

"Okay," I sat down beside him.

"I hear you're leaving tomorrow," he looked down at the ground.

I hadn't realized how upset he was going to get. "We can't stay here forever."

"I know. I thought I would have a little more time is all."

I placed my hand on his shoulder, "I'll miss you too."

He smiled up at me and then shook off my hand. "Come now, let's go to the Commons."

He dragged me to my feet and tossed the ball into a bin. We walked to the Commons, a place where students gathered together and socialized. Some were sipping steaming cups of tea while others were kicking back laughing with friends. I looked around the crowd, I didn't see Thomas' girlfriend.

"No Kyra?" I inquired.

"She's letting me spend time with my friend before she takes off for who knows what adventures," he gave me his most winning smile.

"Nice," I muttered.

He laughed and took a place near one of the crystal windows. We didn't speak much about anything. We chatted about classes, what to expect during the internship, and what it was like to face the Great Seers. Every potential had entered the Temple at least once before becoming a student. Not all Potentials had to face the Great Seers to apply for an internship. Everyone had to stand in front of a panel of Masters, though. This only happened if they were applying early. I had two more years before the natural course of my education would have led me to an internship. I was ready now.

"Do you really have to go on your internship so soon?" he wistfully looked at me.

"I don't fit in here, Thomas," I took his hand in mine. "We both know that."

"You rushed so fast through the classes. You didn't even bother to think some of that energy could have been used to fit in with everyone."

His words stung and I pulled my hand away from him. I was at a loss for words.

"Goodbye Pandria. Peace be with you," he said in a very formal Seer way.

"Peace," tears rolled down my eyes as he swiftly walked away from me. I had been focused on trying to escape from the Centre. I didn't think how it would affect my friendship with Thomas. Maybe someday we would meet again. My heart turned a bit to lead as I left the Common area.

I wandered back to Atheara's. I wasn't paying much attention to where I was going, other than the general direction of my current home.

"Watch where ya going, will you?" an angry voice grumbled.

"Sorry," I raised my eyes to the voice.

"Ya, whatever," she grumbled again. The angry girl had blonde hair and what I guessed used to be blue eyes. These characteristics were the markings of The City child. Her speech indicated a living from the far reaches of the lower outer Community Circles. She was a walking contradiction.

I looked her up and down, searching for other indicators. I saw golden lines encompass this young woman. "What's your problem?" her gray eyes scrutinized me.

"Sorry, I was just trying to figure out where you come from," I blurted out. She smirked at me. "I mean, nothing," I rubbed at my forehead.

"I get it all the time," she hissed.

The confused look on my face must have portrayed my confusion. I tried to keep it neutral, but I couldn't fight the confusion.

She laughed again and walked off. The confusion I felt dissipated. I looked after her, worried I somehow succumbed to another episode. I opened the door and walked straight into Atheara.

"What's wrong, Little One?"

"I'm not sure," I sat down in the Common Area.

She sat crossed legged on the floor. Atheara didn't seem to care much for conventional chairs. "Tell me."

"I was walking home when I ran into a Potential. She was a contradiction. Her appearance seemed to be from The City. Her speech was more from the Lower Outer Communities."

Atheara stayed silent, waiting for more. "Then it was as if I couldn't help myself. I had to be completely honest with her. It's not like I wanted to lie to her or anything. My thoughts were just there for her, a hundred percent accessible," I felt frustrated.

"Her name is Lillith," Atheara said.

"You know her, then?"

"I know of her. I have not met her myself."

"What do you know about her?" I crossed my legs underneath me.

"She was born in The City. Her parents were killed in a horrific accident when she was five. The details are for her to tell, not mine. I know she was adopted to a family in the Outer Communities. She spent another nine years there before coming to The Centre."

"She looked to be about the same age as me," I wondered aloud.

"She is. Her talents developed later than others. She's only been here a couple of years. The Great Seers seem to think they had built up in her. That kind of energy must materialize in some way. In her, it seems to have created an ability to force others to always be honest around her."

"Does this happen often?" I said in awe.

"No, it does not happen often. When a Potential has the ability to have a strong connection with the fatras there is a risk of possible side effects. The power is great and builds. Like a dam, this power threatens to overflow."

I pondered Atheara's words feeling a personal connection to this Lillith. "Little One, it is time for bed," Atheara patted my leg.

"I bet you are going to miss saying that," I chuckled. Her diversion successfully brought me out of my revere. I stood up and stretched. "All right, I will let you boss me around this last time. After tonight you have other Potentials to terrorize." I chuckled. Atheara stood up and hugged me tightly then padded off to her own room.

I pulled on my pajamas and hopped into bed. I pulled the covers tightly around me, breathing in the night air wafting through the open window. My thoughts swirled around the strange girl I had run into. I remembered the abrupt way Thomas had said goodbye to me. I was eager to leave this place behind. I was also sad to leave one of the few friends I had found here in the Centre.

The sun shone brightly the next morning,

throwing rainbow colors throughout my room. I pulled on the Potential clothes I was issued along with the soft soled shoes. Atheara was already gone, probably in her Solar Room. I ate a quiet breakfast in the cafeteria. I went through the departure checklist I received on my way out of the Temple from the previous day. I had to return my cafeteria card. Then I had to go to finance to set up a card for food and lodging while on my internship. I was also going to receive a communication card to contact the Masters whenever I needed. I was to meet my advisor in the auditorium. I was going to be introduced to my mentor who would go with me and guide me for the first few months of my internship. I hoped it wouldn't be the history teacher. I needed someone who could at least keep me awake.

I was able to make it through everything on the checkout list. My meeting with my advisor was not until right after lunch so I meandered over to the cafeteria for my last meal in the Centre. Kyra motioned for me to join her and Thomas. She wasn't usually this inviting. I soon realized the source of her happiness, my departure. She asked an unstoppable flow of questions about my destination and what it was like to speak in the Temple. I kept my responses short. I answered them all the same. It wasn't very often she was nice to me. Thomas remained mute through the meal.

Lunch passed by in a blur. Thomas remained unusually quiet. I didn't push the matter; I was certainly going to miss my closest friend. There were no words I could say to close the gap being created by my early departure from the Centre. He simply waved at me as we went off in different directions, a cloudy expression on his face.

I headed to the auditorium, my advisor waiting for me just outside the doors. The elderly Master waved at me. She hadn't been my original advisor. Most found me a tiresome student, always having to reprimand me for not paying attention in class. She was the most patient and kind. She led me into the large room, curtains hanging down the sides of most of the walls. A stage was arranged in the very front. The chairs were a plush red and comfortable to sit on. We went to the very front and sat in the front row between other Potentials heading out to their internships. There were really only a handful of us. Formality was expected no matter how many were present. To be an intern was an honor. We had to maintain a certain amount of decorum out in the public being the ambassadors of our society.

I didn't recognize any of the other students, most were two grades or more above me. I wasn't much of a socialite. I wouldn't have recognized if someone from my class was in the room. One of the veteran Masters stood on the stage. He spoke to us about honor and dedication to the Seer School. He then went through a list of things which were expected from us and the things we weren't allowed to do. We were not to speak out against the Seer Centre or the Temple. We were always to present ourselves professionally at all times, even when we were not on duty during our internship. This included free time. There was a long speech about consequences. Followed by a short congratulation on our upcoming internships.

I followed my advisor outside. I looked around and saw all the other Potentials greet their mentors. I looked around and saw no one for me. I wondered if maybe my advisor was going to be taking on the responsibility of becoming a mentor when I saw Atheara approach.

"Come to say goodbye?" I grinned.

"Not at all, Little One," she bowed to the Master who bowed back.

"No way!" I exclaimed.

"Don't look so surprised," she eyed me carefully.

"I thought you weren't allowed to leave the Centre?" I hugged her.

"They have granted me permission to be your

mentor. They have recognized our connection and have looked at the fatras. They say our fatras continue to cross. This seems beneficial for us both." Good old Atheara, always getting to the point. I scooped up my bags. I generally felt like I could float all the way to the Second Circle of The Communities. We filed in behind other interns and their mentors and headed to the train station. After storing our things, we found a seat in the General Public Car. With a lurch forward we pulled away from what was once my home, The Seer Centre.

CHAPTER 5:
THE POLITICAL
HOUSE

The distance from the Seer Centre to the Second Community ring was not very far. Atheara had remained silent on the train. I could feel the tension all the interns felt before heading out for the first assignment. We all worried about the amount of responsibility we were taking on. When the train pulled to a stop at the Second Circle depot, Atheara and I pulled our bags from storage and walked away from the track. The train station was large here, being so close to The City and Seer Centre. Maps were posted all over, indicating which train numbers you could take to particular areas of the Second Circle and the times they would arrive. Each circle of Communities contained four Quadrants. We were heading to the Eighth Quadrant of the Second Community.

There were already two Seers in this district

who worked for the citizens here. Each Quadrant usually held at least two Seers and the local Governor communicated to these Seers about any needs they had. The Seers were not just guides for the local politicians. They acted as ambassadors for the Seer Centre. With the Seers, politicians were able to make decisions which steered them away from horrible disputes. This aid meant we were able to avoid wars and civil unrest amongst the citizens.

Atheara pointed down the tracks and held up three fingers. We were to take the Three Train to our Quadrant. There we would walk to the Seer Embassy and take up shelter there. Once we arrived the Seer Ambassador showed us to our room. We were to have adjoining rooms. The setup was similar to what we shared in the Centre: shared living quarters, shared kitchen, and Atheara would have a personal study space. There was no cafeteria out in The Communities. For the first time I would be in charge of feeding myself. I had learned some cooking techniques from Mother. I had never really cooked my own food before.

I tossed my bags on my new bed and took a look around. There was one round window which opened to a fresh herb garden. The smell was rich and reminded me of the rich soil of the Solar Room. I immediately began unpacking, trying to make my new living quarters feel like home. I pinned a picture of Thomas and me up on the wall by a desk along with pictures of my parents. I heard a small tap on my door.

"Dinner, Little One," Atheara smiled. I nodded to her and went to the dining area. She had made a simple herb salad with chicken. We ate in companionable silence. I yawned big. I could distinctly hear her giggle in my head.

"Go, I will clean up," she waved me away. I thought about arguing with her then thought better of it. I went to my room and took one last glance around before darkness enveloped me.

I had vicious dreams. Quadrant Eight was in civil unrest. The streets were burning with a blazing fire. I had just received word my parents had mysteriously vanished. All those in the last ring of The Communities had disappeared as well. I woke up with a start. I had managed to swallow the scream threatening to burst out. Sweat poured down my neck and my hair was a tangled mess. I got up and paced the room, the morning light barely peeking through the window. I finally stopped my pacing and decided to jump into the shower.

Minutes later I was adding the finishing sash of the intern. I walked into the kitchen. Thankfully, they had stocked up on the food in preparation of our arrival and they had been kind to provide a cold cereal choice for breakfast. I ate slowly, thinking over my nightmare. Atheara showed up without a sound. I nearly toppled the table when I realized she was there.

"Rough night?" she eyed me skeptically.

"Bad dreams," I responded through a mouthful of cereal.

"Probably just anxious," she sat down. "We have to meet one of the secretaries as soon as you are done."

I nodded and had trouble swallowing the mouthful of cereal. I was starting to get nervous. I was confident in my skills as a Seer. I was unsure of my ability to handle working with people. Not all Seers became ambassadors, assisting the politicians in each Quadrant. Some remained at the Centre. Some of the Potentials became Masters to teach others the gift of the Seers. Even more spent their lives in study, trying to find new and inventive ways of using our gifts. Atheara once told me the more we expanded our gifts the more anomalies appeared within our group. Anomalies such as the gift Lillith displayed.

I managed to finish my cereal even though my nerves screamed inside me. I grabbed my carrier bag with my tablet in it.

The second ring of The Communities was more compact than I was used to. The Centre, although at the heart of The Communities, gave the illusion there was distance between the dorms and the training rooms. Trees had been plentiful while you wandered around the grounds. Quadrant 8 gave me the opposite feeling. I felt cramped and confined. When I looked out of my temporary room assignment located on the far side of the Political House. My first day there Atheara and I were escorted around the building so we could become accustomed to our surroundings. A low-level secretary was tasked with this job. She made it apparent to us this task was not something she had wanted to be volunteered for.

"Good morning, my name is Karey," she briskly stated. "This morning I am going to show you around the Political House," she marched us away from our new residence. We walked down a long hall to the heart of the Political House. We followed silently behind her as she swept her hand to the left, "This is visitor lodging for those who were sent here from other Quadrants or any of the Elders from The Temple." I saw a cleaning crew in the hall disposing of trash. "This room," she continued on past the visitor hallway to a smallish room behind the visitor Rooms, "is where you will probably be spending most of your time. This is the Seer Office." I peeked inside and saw a modest room filled mostly with books and maps. Orangish light illuminated the room making it seem serene and peaceful. "Next to the office is the supply room. If you are in need of office supplies, you can ask for the key at the receptionist desk or the Resident Seer to obtain access." We then walked past various offices whose inhabitants, by what we were told, assisted with the running of the Political House. Karey stopped close to the receptionist's desk and waved her hand at the big room at the center of the Political House. "This is the conference room where our Governor meets with the various dignitaries from the other Quadrants. I saw stadium type seating inside rising half way up to the ceiling. In the center was a small table which held a 3-D projector. I looked and noticed Karey was chatting to the receptionist, clearly ignoring us.

I stepped inside. "It's curious, isn't it?" I heard Atheara looked around the large room. "Big decisions are made here. Most of the Political Houses are set up the same. Some of the more outlying Quadrants have smaller Houses and Kastor has a much bigger, grander one."

"You've been to Kastor's Political House?" I looked at her seeing wavy lines of gray emanate from her.

"Yes," Atheara turned away from me and headed back to the receptionist desk. I had known Atheara was an unofficial member of the Elders. I hadn't realized they had let her accompany them on official business matters.

"Come along," I heard Karey's clipped tones.

We followed her along the other side of the Political House which contained some more offices, the Governor's grand office, an official residence for any diplomats who came to visit, and of course the Governor's house. She ended the tour at the gardens which I had seen from our small room.

"I have been asked by the resident Seer for you to meet them in the Seer office after lunch today. If you excuse me," she rushed away from us.

"We have not offended her," Atheara's voice echoed softly in my head.

"Get out of my head," I grumbled watching Karey head to one of the offices close to the front door. I sighed and followed glumly behind Atheara to our room. Atheara didn't pry. I knew she was sensing how I was feeling. I hated how people judged me because I looked differently from the other Seers. I wondered how Atheara put up with it with such ease.

"Count to ten, Little One," I heard her as she put down a plate of sandwiches down on the common room table. I began counting in my head as I flopped down on the hard sofa closest to the chair. I laid back, closing my eyes. When I opened them again Atheara had out a tablet and was nibbling on one of the sandwiches. My stomach growled so I picked one up and began munching. My main goal after my orientation with the Political House was to shadow the Seer who was in residence.

After lunch we met the trainer, Gabriel, in the Seer room. Gabriel didn't seem to care too much for me and openly stared at the lines on my face and eyes. Anger boiled close to the surface. I heard Atheara counting inside my head, "One, two, three..." I breathed in deeply and counted to 10. It took five rounds before I forced a smile on my face. Feeling the fakeness of my own smile I attempted to ignore the blatant stares. I was to take notes and only speak when given permission. I was not to interfere with the everyday running of the government.

He described the current Governor of the Eighth Quadrant and what the citizens of this Community were like. Each Quadrant and circle held a main profession. This Quadrant mainly focused on the Physics of Sciences.

"Governor Talland is a shrewd man who focuses on what is best for Quadrant 8. He is also very private. I advise you not to pry or question him," Gabriel stared me down.

I forced myself to do the customary courteous bow and then followed Gabriel. We walked together to the Governor's office. We waited in the foyer for a while before the Secretary showed us in. I bowed to the Governor in the fashion we were trained in the Centre.

"Governor Talland, this is Intern Pandria and her mentor Atheara," Trainer Gabriel smiled at the Governor.

"Light be upon you," I greeted the Governor. His head was devoid of hair completely. Even his eyebrows were gone. His eyes had an intensity about them. He was obviously serious about his duty to the Eighth Quadrant.

"And to you," he robotically replied. He bowed to Atheara, recognizing her rank as Master. The Governor introduced us to some of the secretaries, senators, and other politicians currently residing at the Political House.

Each Quadrant had a visiting representative from other Quadrants and occasionally ambassadors from the other Community Circles. This provided a well-oiled machine which promoted fluent communication between all The Communities. Everyone we met was friendly and spoke in short and brisk sentences, looking up long enough to say hello. After our introductions Governor Talland nodded to the trainer and excused himself stating he had to go back to work. Gabriel showed us back to our work room.

Above light fractured around, casting color everywhere in the room. I looked up and saw the ceiling was made out of carefully crafted crystal, something the Seers seemed to take pleasure in using. I was given my own desk in a corner. Gabriel pulled Atheara aside and when she returned, she was carrying many binders. I glanced at the side of one of them and saw it was a manual for the political structure and the expectations which were placed upon me as an intern. We spent most of the day sifting through the books, reading them carefully. I made some notes on my tablet as we read through them. By late afternoon I was rubbing my eyes to keep them open.

Atheara chuckled, "Okay, enough. It's time for us to be heading back."

I closed the notebook I was poring over and piled them neatly at the corner of my desk. We walked back to the Seer Rooms and ate a light dinner. I flicked on my tablet and looked through my notes again. Atheara had left to meditate outside in the herb garden.

The first month passed by with this rhythm of life. I would wake up, go to the Seer workroom in the Political House, go over books of political procedures, and then return to our new home eating in silence. My brain throbbed from all the information I was stuffing into it. Although we were the guides to a quiet, safe life, our duties extended beyond the political life. We were to appear before the public as symbols of peace and prosperity. The governor was in charge of implementing all rules and governmental procedures throughout the Quadrant they were assigned. This included the specific specialization the Quadrant focused on. Quadrant 8 had a physics focus which was much different than the botany part of science my Mother and I enjoyed. Although I took many science classes both in Academic School and the Seer Centre the area of science this Quadrant focused on was more on an experimental nature. Some of the information was labeled classified and I wondered how I was supposed to assist if I wasn't allowed to know what the residents here were working on. Atheara assured me I only needed to understand the basics to assist the politicians here. The governor depended on the specialists to instruct them.

The second month proved more challenging. I was meeting many of the political figures. For the first few weeks I shadowed Seer Doylle. He was a no-nonsense type of person who didn't really grasp the concept of humor. It was immediately apparent to me I would have to keep to myself around him. Each part of The Communities had their own representatives of police and bankers. However, the Police Sector was operated out of the Second Quadrant where they also ran investigators, judges, and a small jury. The First Quadrant was responsible for the banking system. Over the month I met some of the local area police, secretaries, and bankers.

There was a flow of senators from the other Quadrants and Communities stationed at the Political House as well; each with their own Ambassador Suite. Serious fights rarely broke out between all of the politicians. Their dependency on the Seers assisted them in finding the path of least resistance to maintain harmony and peace. No matter how amicable all appeared to be there were still grating character differences between all involved. Some days I had to force myself to count to ten before looking back up and putting a smile on my face.

Many of the representatives were self-focused while others were so dry in their humor, I was afraid to even smile in their direction. Atheara found my discomfort comical. She always sat on my left side, poking my side whenever she thought I was missing an important point. I wasn't bored with the political process; I was tired of the back-and-forth monotony it took to resolve any issue. A senator would propose an idea to enhance Quadrant Eight, the others would speak in hushed whispers to their Seers. They would then counter the idea based on things they used in their own Communities and the senator would speak to his or her Seer. The verbal battle would bounce back and forth for days and only be resolved until all parties were satisfied. I understood the importance of the process, even if it was tedious, and I was told it was much better than the old days.

I was starting to fret over losing the company of Atheara. Most mentors spent the first couple of months with the intern. She told me half way through the second month she was going to stay on at the Political House. I tried to inquire as to why they would change the rules. She refused to answer me. I wondered if she was staying for my safety or to keep me in line.

A couple more months passed by of tedious studying and observing. Just when I thought I couldn't stuff in any more information in my tired brain I was finally assigned my first duty. I was to be the Seer to the local police group.

They often used Seers to determine the correct path to assist a small-time criminal back onto the path of being a contributing member of our society. I could see the choices which would bring the person back to the crime and which choices would help them avoid criminal activity. I had learned from Doylle to keep my responses short and to the point. I tapped all my interactions with the police group into my tablet using forms on the general folder server so Atheara and other Masters could log in to review my work if any problems arose. Other Seers could determine if what I saw was correct or if somehow a mistake was made. I didn't make many mistakes and none of them were certainly anything worth reporting to The Centre or The Temple. I sometimes suggest a path which I knew would be a rougher choice than some other decisions would have been.

One time I was called in to sit in on an interrogation between a weathered worn Miner who had wandered further into The Communities looking for easy money. Beggars were not welcomed in The Communities. You were supposed to be a contributing member. There was no other choice. I could see how he had struggled working in the mines. His fatras were before him. If he was to be sent back to the mines, he would end up a repeat offender. If he was given the choice to be given a different work task in another Quadrant, he would become an effective member of The Communities. However, I suggested a third option which the fatras were a murky color when I looked upon them. This path took him back to the mines in a guidance position rather than hard labor. I was uncertain if he would revert back to his old ways. In the end, I chose to go with the middle road as my suggestion in the hopes he could lend his knowledge of the mines to those who could use his expertise. The Mining Guild later reported that although he had an occasional argument with the workers in the mines, he had not tried to escape back into other

Quadrants. My advice proved to be valuable. He had gone on to save the life of some miners in a tunnel he had deemed unsafe. Had I gone with the easier choice those workers may have perished in the collapsed tunnel. Overall, the police force seemed happy with my work.

A routine developed which included spending quality time with Atheara. She taught me how to play chess without the use of our skills. I began to take up drawing as a way to overcome stress. Atheara taught me how the different herbs could be used for medical purposes. She was very adept at medicinal herbs, almost as good as my own Mother.

"Do you think we make a difference?" I casually asked her as I moved a pawn across the holographic board.

She pondered my question, moved a bishop, and then responded, "I think we make an impact in The Communities; sometimes good, sometimes bad."

"Sometimes bad?" I scrunched up my eyes.

"Think about it, Pandria," Atheara insisted.

"Are you saying we control the fates too much?" We had this discussion many nights before and it was a subject we constantly returned to. "The Elders don't think so otherwise they would recall us all."

"It's true we keep the peace. There's always a consequence to our actions, good or bad," Atheara insisted. "For instance, I can move my queen here and take your bishop but then I would expose her to the rook. True, I would eliminate the threat he poses to my king but everything is interconnected."

I looked down at the board in wonderment. I didn't disagree with her. I wanted to hold onto the belief what we did here helped keep the peace.

"I agree, Little One. Enough of this deep talk. It's time for bed."

I nodded, "Thank you for the game, Atheara." She smiled and patted my head. I padded off to my room.

I lay there for a long time, thinking over her words. Every action has an opposite and equal reaction. That's one of the things I learned at the Academy before being sent to the Centre. I knew Atheara was right but surely using our "gift" meant we were able to make the opposite reaction just as positive as our own actions.

I was due for a visit to my family. I had not seen them for months. Working at the Political House didn't allow as much visiting time as it did when I was a Potential at the Centre. I often wondered how Thomas and Kyra were doing. The idea of missing Kyra confused me.

Atheara announced to me I was to be given a week to go visit my family. She would be going back to the Centre while I was away. We packed our things and said our goodbyes at the station. I was old enough now to travel home without the need of my Father joining me. I missed his company, though. Without our companionable silence I was left to my own which proved to be a dangerous thing. Unwanted thoughts crept into my head and seeped into my heart. I was unsure of my place as a Seer and replayed all mistakes I had made. By the time I arrived at my home Community Circle and rode the train over to our Quadrant I was in a brooding mood. Father's smile pulled me out of my funk. I happily entered our house. I immediately noticed a big difference. The carefully tended plants were running wild. There was no aroma of delicious food. I sat my bags down by the door and looked at Father quizzically.

"Pandria, we need to speak," words a daughter never wants to hear from either one of her parents.

I numbly sat down at the table and squeezed my hands together.

"Something has happened. Will, I'm not exactly sure what has happened if you want the honest truth."

"Father," I placed my hand on top of his.

"Mother has disappeared," he blurted out. "She was out with the botanist group just on the outer skirt of our Community. She never returned. None of them did. The Seers have been informed of this. They are all trying to figure out where they went and what happened."

"How can that happen?" I gaped. "I thought having Seers prevented stuff like this from happening."

"They try their best Pandria. We are all human," Father sighed.

"But," I began.

"Buts don't change what has happened, Pandria. We will find your Mother, somehow," Father sounded more like he was trying to reassure himself.

"Maybe if I speak to our Governor it would help," I tried to offer.

"They are doing all they can, Pandria. I understand your need to do something proactive to help. For now, we must stay positive."

"Why didn't the Seers tell me?" I started crying.

"They didn't want to upset you. The Elders

thought it best if I told you," Father got up and hugged me. I could smell lavender on his skin and immediately missed Mother. I swallowed down the fear which crept into my throat. I put on a brave face for Father. He saw right through me of course and in his style, he tried to show courage, too, as he smiled back.

I held him close for a while then let go. I picked up my bag and headed for my room. Plopping on the bed fully clothed, I lay there for a while. Atheara had warned me looking past The Communities might cause more damage to me. I decided not looking might do more damage than good in regard to finding Mother. I would start with our Community first and work my way through all The Communities. I would go past them if I had to in order to find her.

I cleared my mind and stared at the last of the sunlight filtering through my window. I saw the lines of fatras swirl all around me. I followed them out the window and to the edge of the Community Quadrant we lived in. I didn't see Mother anywhere. The lines were blurry here. I pushed myself further and tried to clearly see the fatras. The left was a bleak blackness, the right was a hazy red, while the middle was slightly clearer. This fatras line was more like muddled water than a clear fatras line. I followed the Fate Line. The more I pushed towards the Barrens the more searing hot pain burned within my mind. I finally let go of the sight and I sat in bed, sweat running down my head. My face burned bright. I glanced in a mirror and saw the golden threads on my cheeks and in my eyes glow brightly.

After not finding any sign of Mother I closed my eyes and fell into an exhaustive sleep. I had the worst nightmare. I couldn't recall any of the details and woke up screaming. Father was there, cradling my head in his lap trying his best to soothe me. I finally quit screaming and slowed my breathing which was ragged, tears stung my cheeks. I was at least calm enough to sit up.

"What is it?" Father's concern creased his forehead.

"I don't know, Father," I was out of breath.

"Do I need to call the Seers?" the look of concern etched into his face.

"No, I think I am all right."

He looked concerned. I didn't elaborate on what had happened. He stayed with me until I fell asleep. Just his presence brought me comfort.

The next morning the light dimly sifted through my window. I groggily rubbed at my eyes. I still couldn't recall the nightmare. I knew it had something to do with Mother. My fears of her fate had crept into my dreams.

"Morning, Pandria. Are you feeling better?" Father flipped an egg.

"You know how to cook?" I tried to interject some humor back into our lives.

"I can cook, clean, and take care of the house," he quipped.

"We shall see," I smiled as he slid the eggs onto my plate. They were nothing like Mother's cooking, and barely passed as edible. A knock resounded on our door as I slid the clean plates back into their cupboards.

"Good morning," Atheara's familiar voice swept into my mind.

"You called Atheara?" I was angry at my Father.

"Yes, you scared me last night. I've never seen you this bad before Pandria," he reprimanded.

"I'm fine, Atheara. I'm sorry you've come all this way for nothing," I stated aloud for the benefit of Father.

"I will determine if you are fine," Atheara stressed the last word.

She motioned for me to follow. We entered Mother's garden at the back of the house. I sat crossed legged on the ground. Atheara sat across from me. I placed my palms up and let her place her hands against mine. We closed our eyes and I felt her following my fatras.

"You have been looking past The Communities again," Atheara said as a matter of fact statement rather than an accusation. "You were looking for your Mother," she continued. "Your search took you past The Communities and almost burned you," she lowered her hands. "I do not blame you, Little One, for looking for your Mother. You must be more careful. We already know looking past The Communities is dangerous for you; maybe for all of us."

"Yes Master," I ground my teeth.

Atheara stared at me for a while and then sighed. "Let us try together," she finally said.

"I thought you said it would be dangerous for me to look past The Communities."

"Without guidance, yes," There was a long pause before she simplistically stated, "Let us try together."

I closed my eyes. I could feel her presence beside my own. We searched down through the fatras to the edge of my home Quadrant. I saw once again the blurred crystalline line going straight. We were able to reach The Barrens this time without any pain. Our way was blocked. Together we couldn't penetrate the unseen wall.

"There is nothing more we can see right now," Atheara opened her eyes.

"She is lost, then?" I asked.

"We will not give up," she patted my hand.

Father came out, concern shimmering in his eyes. He insisted Atheara stay in his room while he slept on the couch. Father and I visited with each other while she meditated. In the morning, Atheara and I visited the Political House in our Quadrant to find out how the investigation was going. She made me swear upon my duty as a Seer not to go looking at the fatras past The Communities without her again. I grudgingly agreed.

The temptation to search for Mother pressed upon me. I felt my thoughts fill with this very thought in both my waking and sleeping hours. I had to force a part of myself to spend time with Father and listen to his words. I didn't want to insult him by not hearing something he said. I knew he was equally worried, and the strain could be seen around his usually carefree eyes.

"What should we do today?" he asked.

I shook my head while I nibbled at the rubbery eggs, he placed in front of me.

"I'm still not the greatest chef, I admit defeat,"

he laughed for the first time since I arrived.

His laughter was contagious and before I could stop myself, I was caught up in a giggle fit. The laughter only died when Atheara knocked on the door.

"Hello Atheara," I said somberly.

"Hello to you, too, Little One," she snarked.

"Sorry, it's not you,"

"Really?" I heard the titter of laughter in her inner voice. "It's not you, it's me excuse?"

"You know that's not how I meant it," I chided.

Father just looked at us. I kept forgetting how awkward it might seem to him when we spoke with just our minds instead of our voices like other normal people. I shook my head and dumped the rest of breakfast in the sink.

"What brings you back so early?" I said aloud to Atheara. I was hoping her trek to the Political House this morning brought hope.

"I bring news," she sat down at the table.

"Father, she says she brings news."

"What is it Atheara?" I said simultaneously in my head.

"We are heading to the edge of the Outer

Communities in Quadrant 24 to look for your Mother's group." She got to the point as she usually did.

"She has been found?" I jumped up to my feet. Father looked up hopefully then placed his hand upon my shoulder.

"There's more, I think" he pointed to Atheara.

"What is it, Atheara?"

"Quadrant 24 was the last spot your Mother's group was last seen. They are not sure if they are still there or not. The Masters and Great Seers both agree our fatras lead us in this direction." I relayed the message to Father. For the first time since I arrived, I saw a genuine smile on his face.

"Then what are we waiting for?" I jumped up and ran to my room. I began to throw some clothes into my bag along with my tablet which held all the notes I had ever collected during my studies. I paused, realizing I was supposed to return to the Political House to resume my duties. I threw the bag over my shoulder and tossed a coat over my arm. I walked back out to the kitchen where I left Atheara. Father was gone. She was calmly sitting there.

"What about my internship?" I hesitantly asked.

"They have given you a deferred leave until

this matter has some sort of resolution."

"Meaning I have to return whether or not we find my Mother," I read between the lines.

"Yes," She said. I appreciated Atheara never lied to me.

"There's something you are holding back?"

"We need to take along someone. I know you aren't really good at strangers. Your progress at the Political House may help us in this case."

"Who?"

"Lillith."

"The strange girl who makes you speak the truth?"

"Yes. The Great Seers feel she would benefit our search as we look in the last circle of The Communities. They don't trust insiders as much as their own. Lillith would give us the advantage."

"She creeps me out," I grumbled.

"Who creeps you out, darling?" Father had a pack slung over his back.

"Lillith," I slumped.

Father eyed me critically. "This may be too much for Pandria. Maybe we should send her back to the Political House or even The Centre."

"Not a chance Dad," I slapped his shoulder playfully and walked outside, avoiding a fight about me coming along on this search. I knew sitting around at either the Political House or Centre would drive me crazy. I would be more tempted to look past the boundaries just to be sure no one else I cared about disappeared on me. The sun shone brightly with thick clouds billowing in the sky just to the south. I set my bag down and pulled on my coat.

"Is everyone almost ready?" a familiar voice inquired.

"Yes," came out of my mouth before I could stop it. I rolled my eyes.

"Look, I'm not very eager to go out into the Outer Circle either. I left there for a reason."

"Could you just not radiate the sense for everyone to always tell the truth? Rein it in or something?"

"Can you stop having those freakish lines all around your face?"

"Fair enough," I looked back at the house. Father came ambling out with Atheara behind him.

"Behave, both of you," she scolded us.

"This is me behaving," I looked at the ground.

"Do you want to return to The Centre?"

I looked up at the road and started walking toward the train. I knew her threats were a bit on the empty side. However, I didn't want to push her too far.

Father walked beside me, chatting with me while letting his gaze slide over to Lillith. She smiled wide at me. I shook my head. Her smile was cheesy statement of 'you're stuck with me now what are you going to do?' look.

The train station to the Outer Community was empty. No one really traveled out towards the last rings of The Communities unless they had to. Most of the residents in the Outer Circle never really liked traveling inward, either.

CHAPTER 6: QUADRANT TWENTY-FOUR

The rain poured as we pulled away from home. Drips left silver streaks upon the train window. My breath was fogging it up as I pressed my forehead upon the glass, feeling its smooth surface on my forehead. Being around Lillith gave me a headache. I had to put forth all my will not to blurt out any and all information I had since I was a baby. Father must have felt the effects, too. He was telling her about Mother; how they met, where their first kiss was, and other such intimate details a daughter didn't need to hear. Lillith must have sensed this as well. For a while, she remained an intent audience. She finally excused herself and walked down to the opposite end of the train.

"How does she handle it?" I asked Atheara mentally.

"How do you handle your gift?" She asked.

"Yes, but others aren't always prattling on to me."

"You always see their possible paths."

"I still say her gift is more of a challenge."

"You may want to ask her about it."

"And how do I control just saying whatever truths are in my head?"

"Concentration, thought before speaking, and patience."

I sighed and nodded at Atheara. I found Lillith at the far end of the train, tracing her fingers along the path of the water drops from the rain outside.

"What do you want?"

I felt the tug of needing to speak without thinking. I stopped myself, biting my cheek in the process. I breathed in deeply, using the breathing techniques I had used back at the Centre. "I wanted to know how you put up with everyone spilling out their guts to you."

A smile tugged at the corner of Lillith's mouth, "A lot of patience I guess."

I wanted to say it didn't look like she had much

patience. I breathed in deeply again and said instead, "Do you listen to what they say, or do you just let them keep on talking without paying attention to them?"

This time Lillith actually looked amused. "I listen. One of the side effects of my gift," she stressed the last word.

"Wow, sounds tedious," I blurted out.

Lillith rolled her eyes. She remained silent and pointedly stared out the window. I counted backwards from ten this time, "Were you born with this gift?"

Lillith eyed me critically, "I'm not sure. I wasn't aware of it until I was fourteen. That's when my foster parents sent me to the Centre."

"I was ten when my parents sent me."

"Was that when your eyes changed?" Lillith leaned forward a little.

"I fainted in front of the Great Seers and was unconscious for a while. Atheara helped me when I regained consciousness," I felt the tug of the robotic answer try to come out. I managed to make it sound conversational.

Lillith grinned this time. She leaned back and brushed back a piece of her blonde hair. "I heard about your time in the hospital from a girl at The

Centre, Kyra. A friend of yours?" she smirked.

"A girlfriend of my friend Thomas," I corrected her. I sat back and gazed out the window. The last of my Quadrant passed by and we were passing through a ring of forest before the last Community Ring; one of the designs of the founders. They wanted to bring a bit of nature back to our lives. Our ancestors designed it so each Community Ring had some kind of vegetation and nature between them.

"It's beautiful," Lillith mused.

"Yes," I agreed.

We remained silent for the rest of the ride. Lillith was less inept at socializing than I was. I at least tried with people, even though there were only a few. She was reserved and skeptical. I considered the irony since people were forced to always tell her the truth. Maybe she didn't trust their sincerity. I was curious about Lillith and not just because of her unique ability to bring out the truth in others. She was a paradox.

I must have fallen asleep. Atheara was shaking my arm. I rubbed at my eyes and noticed the train had come to a stop. I pulled the bag over my shoulder and then followed Father onto the platform. The air felt staler here, suppressing. A thick fog encompassed the area. I could see the sun trying to pierce through the thickness. The light was foreign and radiated through the horrible air.

"Take short breaths, Pandria," Father instructed.

The constriction felt irritating. Shallow breaths felt better than taking a deep breath. I wondered how I would use my breathing techniques to cope here.

"We will have to devise another," Atheara answered for me.

"Out of my mind," I thought back at her. I looked around, "Where do we go from here?"

"What does Atheara say?" Father turned back to me.

"Well?" I asked her.

"The Political House, they have rooms set up for us courtesy of the Centre."

"Which way?"

She pointed a long finger to the train to the left of us. Father nodded and we walked over to the train, boarding it just before it left. We zipped around to the Political House. The air was no better here. The houses were run down, the paint chipping in many places.

"Why are they living like this?" I wondered

aloud.

"They have very little choice in the matter," Lillith's voice seethed.

I looked up and only now remembered her foster family lived here.

"I'm sorry, Lillith. I didn't mean to be rude. I just don't understand why the same standards in other Quadrants aren't the same here."

Lillith pulled my arm forcing me to look at her. "Not all of us are fortunate. Not everyone is as important as a Seer or has inflated egos like a politician. They live simply, and with purpose. They don't care for style, frills, or other unnecessary distractions. They live to serve the Seer Centre and politicians. In return they want protection and the bare essentials to live life comfortably."

This idea seemed very strange to me. All anyone could talk about in my Quadrant was how they wished they could be like the City Center with grand shops, buildings with style and flourish. The idea to live a simple life was just pointless. One should always work to better their life. I held my thoughts to myself. I was certain Atheara heard my thoughts. She looked at me critically. She didn't speak to me. I bowed my head. I was feeling ashamed for some reason but not understanding why.

We reached the Political House quickly. We

walked only a few rows down from the train station. The Political House had more style than all the buildings put together in Quadrant 24. The building looked out of place here. The Seer in residence opened the door before Atheara could knock. She motioned for us to come in.

"Good evening," she walked us through the building. "We have set up a suite of rooms for you all. Pandria and her Father will share one set of rooms and Lillith and Atheara will share the other set. You will share a common area. There is only one kitchen here, unfortunately. We all share it. Your suite has one bathroom between all of you as well. We are a modest Political House and we have made it comfortable. Atheara, the garden is small and is located through a door on the east wing if you wish to meditate there." Without another word the Seer showed us around our temporary home. After she was finished, she quietly slipped out the door to the suite. I didn't really feel the need to put anything away, knowing we would only be here until Mother was found.

"Hungry, kiddo?" Father asked.

"For your cooking, no," I smiled sweetly.

"Ha, ha," he laughed as I closed the door to my bedroom. There was only a slit of a window which was made of glass. The light was already beginning to fade. The fog distorted the light. I could only sense its descent. I didn't dare try to follow the fatras this close to the Outer Ridge without Atheara.

I pulled on my pajamas and flopped into bed. I stared at the ceiling until sleep took over.

"Mother!" I called out. "Where are you?"

I saw shadows in the fog. Just outlines really. I thought I could possibly see Mother's figure in the murky darkness.

"Is that you?" I asked again. The fatras streaked past me, ringing out as they jetted past. They were the only sound around as everything else was mute. "Mother!" I called out again.

My voice echoed. I tried to walk forward. I was stopped by an unseen wall. I felt a burning sensation and I screamed in agony. Backing away I collapsed to the ground, crying for Father who was nowhere to be seen. Through tears pouring from my eyes, I saw the fatras hit the unseen wall. The fatras burned red hot, disappearing in ash.

"Wake Little One!" Atheara was yelling.

I opened my eyes which burned. My hands felt blistered. "What?" I started.

"Hush now, you are safe. You have not drunk your tea before sleeping, have you?" her voice chided.

I shook my head. I did not want to utter a sound as my throat burned. I felt Lillith pull me to a sitting position and Father grabbed my other side, helping her. I laid my head back against the wood panel of the headrest. My temples pounded.

Atheara coaxed my mouth open. I felt warm liquid drizzle into my mouth. The burning sensation in my throat lessened. I could hear past the pounding in my head. I hadn't realized while they were sitting me up and pouring the herbal tea down my throat, I could hear the lullaby Mother usually sang to me coming from Atheara. I wondered where she learned the song. I remembered she had been there in the hospital when I was first taken ill. The pain started to subside. Darkness swept me into a gentle slumber.

I wasn't sure how long it had been since the horrible dream. A ghostly light filtered through. My forehead still felt warm. I was able to open my eyes. My mouth felt dry, as if I hadn't had any water in weeks. There was a tall glass on my bedside table. I drank it down with a little too much enthusiasm, water dripping down my shirt front. I set the glass down and noticed scars on my hands. I looked at them. Etched into them were the same golden lines I had on my cheeks. How on earth I managed to follow the fatras in my sleep was beyond me. All Seers had to consciously follow the Fate Lines. I couldn't remember any stories of anyone following them in their sleep.

I got out and pulled out fresh clothes from my bag. My hands shook as I pulled them on. Flashes of the dream which had seared my hands invaded my thoughts. I hastily tried to push them aside. I flipped open my tablet and looked at a schematic of Quadrant 24. There were a few shops close to the Political House. On the far south side was a Science Center. Past the Science Center stood a small Academia. Next to it were a series of storage units to hold the precious metal mined from the Outer Ridges. This was the bulk of work in the last circle of the Communities. The Science Center was just an outlet building and was well known for examining the conditions in the Outer Ridges. They studied ways to improve the hazardous conditions beyond our walls. The wars had brutally ravaged the land and left many deep scars where even vegetation wasn't growing. I saw the ring of trees just outside the last circle of our civilization. Just beyond was a tall wall made of the same metal mined from the Outer Ridges. Four gates were manned by small armies. These gates protected us from any outside threat though anyone or anything willing to come into The Communities probably couldn't exist beyond the wall. I closed my tablet and placed it in my bag which I slung over my shoulder. I walked out to the Common area and found it empty with a note from Father, "In the dining area". I exited our suites and made my way there. The smell of food didn't seem very appetizing. I sat down at the table where Lillith was swallowing eggs without chewing.

"How are you, Little One?" Atheara sat down beside me.

"Tired," I said before I could stop myself. I looked up at Lillith and knew I didn't have the strength to fight her gift today. She scowled at me and stalked off to the kitchen where I could hear pans clatter. Father must be in there hiding away from me.

I placed my head against the table. "Go back to bed, Little One. I will come get you if we find anything."

"Not a chance," I said to the ground.

"You are in no shape, Pandria," she chided.

"I'm not staying here," I looked up to glare at her. She grabbed my hands. I involuntarily yanked them back.

"You were burnt in your dream," Atheara looked at me with shock. "What was it you were dreaming of?"

I realized she didn't know the truth. I had felt

it might be possible I had followed the fatras in my sleep. With her surprised look I realized this to be the truth. I was glad Lillith had left the room. I didn't want to give it away. "I don't know how it happened. My hands are already healing," I showed my palms to her while trying to conceal the new golden lines already starting to show up.

"I can tell you are holding back from me?" Atheara looked puzzled.

I tried to clear my mind the best I could and looked at her, "Of course not," I tried to give her my best smile.

A look of concern shadowed her eyes. She didn't question me further.

"Hey, you're up!" Father called. "Here, eat up," he placed a plate of eggs in front of me. I tried to look cheerful as I pretended to eat. I mostly pushed the food around the plate. He didn't seem to notice. His attention was focused on plans to find Mother and her botany group. He avoided looking at my hands. As he passed by the table, I could see concern cross across his face.

"We should start at the Science Center," he told Atheara.

Lillith translated for him, "She says your suggestion is a good idea. If we can figure out what she was doing out here we might be able to figure out where they were going."

"I was thinking the same thing. Has anyone here given you any information on what they were doing?" He asked her.

Lillith looked at Atheara then back at Father, "No, they seem to think they were sent from the Science Center in your Quadrant. All Mrs. Arturas' group reported was they were doing plant studies found at the very edge of the last Community."

"If it were something simple, wouldn't she have just told you, Dad?"

"I don't know. She sent me a message saying she would have to travel and would be home late. She told me not to wait up."

Mom often worked late. This was nothing new. She was a part of a group in charge of figuring out how to stimulate plant growth in the Outer Ridge. She often tended to the gardens in our Quadrant. She was constantly working in the lab to create an environmental resistant plant, one which could withstand harsh conditions while still being rich enough in vitamins to sustain life. Thinking about this I lost the thread of the conversation. I was confused why they were all staring at me.

"Um, yes?" I asked.

"Atheara was asking if you wanted to sit with

her at the Science Building to see if you can follow the fatras to find her. Maybe Lillith should be the one," Father looked apprehensive.

"I want to do it," I blurted out. I bit my lip and avoided looking at Lillith. I really had to get my head cleared. I wanted to control myself around her.

"If you're sure?" Father skeptically looked at me. He glanced at Atheara, intensely scrutinizing her facial features to see doubt or a hint I shouldn't help in this endeavor. He must have not found what he was looking for. He bowed his head in defeat. I took a small bite of the food Father had offered me. Restless won over and I stood up, "What are we waiting for?"

"Okay, Little One, we'll go," Atheara stood up and slung a bag over her shoulder.

The air outside was stifling. I took short breaths, my shoulders slightly moving to my labored breaths. Atheara had mastered more control than I and appeared a more relaxed in her attempts to take shorter breaths.

"This way" Atheara nodded toward the train station. Although the outer Communities were less crowded it took a longer arc around the circle to reach certain destinations. The inside of the train offered some respite to the sandpaper air outside.

"I do not like this, Little One," Atheara scowled at me.

"I'm fine, I promise," I focused my gaze on my hands.

She studied me as the train bumped along. It pulled into our stop. We hopped off looking for the Science Building.

We entered through wood paneled doors. The building was small. There was a bustle of sound throughout the building.

"Good day, Mr. Arturas, Intern Pandria," a scientist in a lab coat bowed to us. "And these two must be Master Kinnet and Potential Lillith?" he greeted them.

Father shook his hand, "Thank you for letting us take a look around."

"To be honest, I thought the Seer Guild would be the only ones here. The more eyes the better," he shrugged.

We passed by some labs and computer stations. I noticed there were only a few people in each room as I took a peek through small circular windows looking into each of the rooms. In the 8th Quadrant, the Science Building held many employees, making the space feel small and cramped. Here, there seemed to be an abundance of room. We entered a bio dome in the epicenter of the building, light streamed from the ceiling.

A line of desks was pushed up against one of the walls. The remainder of space was filled with colorful flowers and bright, green leaves. Tendrils of vines swept around bulky stalks. Nothing like I had ever seen in the Centre.

"Here are the botanists' notes they left behind. Not much to go on since they took their tablets with them. We are trying to access their files. It seems they have them locked. Their equipment is not traceable through our normal methods of tracking."

"And the police?" Lillith eyed the scientist.

He looked at her nervously, seeming to feel the aura of truth I always felt with her. Non-Seers might feel her powers and didn't understand them like the gifted did. "They have given up," He blurted.

"What?" Father's eyes blazed.

"I'm sorry, Sir. I didn't mean to just come out and say it like that," he put up both hands.

"I think you better explain," I spat.

From the corner of my eye, I noticed Lillith backing away from all of us.

"They said there was nothing more they could

do. They were going to let you know eventually but thought you should take a look around, first. They were handing the case over to the Seers."

"And they expect us to do their job!" I yelled.

"Pandria, enough," Atheara's voice commanded.

I bit my lip. I knew I crossed the line of professionalism. This involved my own Mother. I turned away and saw the lines streaking throughout the entire room. When my emotions became overloaded, I couldn't help but see all the fatras. I had to calm myself down, counting to fifty before seeing things normally again. I envisioned my bubble encasing me, blocking out all my senses to the fatras. My heart slowed down to a manageable pace. I caught the last exchange between the scientist and Father.

"Thank you, we will take a look around and take it from here."

I saw the man exit the room. Lillith was combing through the scraps of paper on the desk. Atheara was patting Father's arm. He shook his head and then looked around the room.

"Better?" She eyed me critically.

I nodded. "Where should I start?"

"Maybe you and Atheara should try your

meditation thing?" Father looked over his shoulder. Lillith looked up from her searching briefly and then turned her back to us.

Atheara waved at me. We walked to the middle, sitting across from each other on the cold, concrete floor. I relaxed my gaze and felt Atheara's presence beside my own. I could feel the paths of others who had been in this room. We carefully traced them back to their owners. After sifting through many of these fatras I felt a hand on my shoulder.

"Time to stop for tonight," Father said. The light was fading, an orange glow filling the room.

I hadn't realized we had been following the fatras all day. We even skipped lunch. My stomach grumbled loudly.

"Guess you are hungry enough to eat even my cooking," Father forced a laugh out. He helped Atheara up who seemed to be drained more than I felt. She leaned heavily on Father as we headed back to the Political House. We ate a quiet dinner and then all drifted off to bed. I was so tired I really didn't have the energy to try to hold a conversation.

Atheara and I returned to the Science Building and sat upon the floor, sifting through fatras line after fatras line. The second day we followed a promising line only to discover it was the police who had been searching for Mother. Each person had a unique aura despite fatras lines having the distinct clear, cloudy, or red line. I didn't see Mother's distinguishable aura amongst the many which threaded through the Science Building. I hadn't thought so many people had come out this far in The Communities.

We did this for a couple weeks, threading through all the fatras. Father had found a couple of leads and took Lillith with him as he searched the very edge of Quadrant 24. They found a couple of people who saw her group looking around the area. None of them saw anything more.

"I don't know if we will find them," I exhaled.

"We will, Little One," Atheara patted my knee. "How is your head?" she looked up concerned.

"I haven't had any other episodes."

"You know it comes from a place of caring."

"I know." Every day she asked the same questions, worried I would follow the fatras too far. "Wait," I held up my hand. She didn't question me which meant she might have seen it, too. "There it is," I got excited. I followed the familiar line of my Mother. There were a couple other lines which paralleled hers. These must be the other members of the research group. The lines went out of the building to the far Northern

Quadrant, intersecting with people as they went. They stayed in the Northern part for a while and then looped back and forth between the Science Building and Northern Quadrant. I felt a familiar hand on my shoulder before I could follow it any further. I shuddered at the touch.

"Father, we found it!"

"Did you find her?" He excitedly asked.

Atheara looked up at Lillith who responded for her, "Not yet."

"Come, Pandria."

"We are so close!"

"Pandria, you are no help to your Mother if you are so exhausted you can't see straight," Father scolded me for the first time since I was a young child.

I looked down, tears rolling down my cheeks. "Pandria, you can't push yourself so far you risk injuring yourself or becoming sick."

I looked up into his worried eyes. I never thought about how he felt when we went searching through the fatras. He had been with me for several of the episodes. I hadn't considered he was afraid for me.

"He's right, Little One," Atheara stood up and proffered her hand to me. I grunted and stood up.

We walked in silence back to the Political House. Father and I were entering the House when I saw a woman in slacks waving at me. Dirt was wiped down the front of her shirt. I glanced at Atheara and Father then back at her. Lillith followed my gaze and nodded at me.

"Be right back," she called to them.

We walked over to the woman who was leaning into the shadows. "Can we help you?" Lillith inquired.

"Good evening," her hoarse voice whispered.

"How can we help you?" Lillith folded her hands in front of her.

"You're looking for the science group?" She looked at us.

"Yes," she invited the woman to continue.

"They were sent to the northern section. In reality, they were being set up," she clapped her hands over her mouth.

This was the one time I was glad Lillith was with me. This conversation would probably have gone a lot slower without her.

"What do you mean?" I eyed her critically.

"She was sent there by those in the Political House. They have been scouting the area for months, maybe even years."

"You think they are looking for something?" Lillith questioned.

"Possibly," she shrugged.

"Why would they make them disappear? Did they find what they were looking for?"

"Not that I know of. They headed out to the northern part of town and never returned."

I bit my lower lip, trying hard not to accuse this person of over dramatizing what could have been a harmless act. I looked at the fatras and realized my negativity would only worsen the situation. Taking a deep breath, I said, "Do you know who put in the order for the botany group to scout the northern section specifically?"

She nervously looked around, "I would ask the Governor of this Quadrant your question." She clapped her hands over her mouth.

"We're asking you," Lillith sneered.

"You've bewitched me!" She hissed. "You're with them."

"No!" I waved my arms at her, trying to stop her from fleeing to no avail. She sprinted for the train station and disappeared amongst the crowd of people.

"That was pointless," Lillith sighed and stomped into the Political House.

I stared off in the distance, trying to follow the strange woman's fatras. Her Fate Lines unraveled as I reached the station.

"Everything all right?" Father put an arm around my shoulder as I entered our suite.

I nodded, looking out the window. Darkness had come early, the lights of the lamps barely illuminating the rooms. Atheara had already retired to her room.

Father slid a plate of sandwiches across the table to me. I ate silently, enjoying the company of my Father who chatted about the notes Mother's group had left behind.

"There were notes on various brushes they had found at the border with a couple notes on some trees struggling to grow in the Outer Ridges."

"Nothing more?" I looked up at him.

"Why?"

"I don't know," I tried to push his question aside. Exhaustion hit me. I quickly cleaned up. "Just wish there were some real reason why she's gone. Something we could use to find her."

"I know how you feel Pandria," Father hugged me.

"Sleep well tonight."

"You too, Father."

I went to bed. I began the breathing exercises I learned at the Centre. As usual it lulled me into a deep sleep. I had my regular tea mixture while eating dinner, so no dreams came to me. Peace at last.

The next day brought a thick fog, dew drops sticking to the glass of the windows. Father had waited for me in the communal kitchen while the others were already outside the Political House.

"Now we are alone, Pandria, tell me the truth. What is bothering you?" Father sat across from me.

I chewed slowly on the toast I had been trying to get down for the last five minutes. "What do you mean?"

"Don't give me that," he placed both his hands upon the table. "Truth, now."

I looked up at him and decided to give in, "There was this woman yesterday who spoke to Lillith and me. She didn't come right out and accuse the government. However, I believe she seems to think the Political House had something to do with Mother's disappearance."

"Don't be absurd," Father looked at me intently.

"It wasn't my theory, Father," I scowled.

He shrugged, "Sorry Pandria. I asked for the truth. I believe you. What did she look like?"

"She had her face covered by a hood and stood in shadows. I didn't get a real good look at her face. She wore slacks and she looked like she lived outside rather than indoors."

"Could be someone from the Science Center," Father mused. "Was she perhaps with the group Mother had been with?"

"She didn't say," I looked thoughtfully at Father. I oftentimes forgot how observant he truly was. "I wish you had been there when we talked to her. You are good at observing the tiny details and ask the obvious questions."

Father laughed at this. "Thank you, Pandria."

We cleaned up quickly and walked outside, looking around the garden for Atheara and Lillith who were nowhere in sight.

"Maybe they are following a lead."

"Without leaving a note?"

"Possibly."

"I'm going to go ask around to see if anyone has seen them."

Father nodded and followed me back into the Political House. We agreed to look all over the Political House and meet back at our suite.

"Have you seen Atheara and Lillith?" I inquired at the front desk. The man sitting there just shook his head and went back to the papers spread across the desk.

"How about you?" I questioned a woman passing by the front desk. She shook her head as she rushed past.

I spent a good ten minutes in this fashion, asking anyone within earshot. No one had seen them. I was sitting outside the Governor's office, waiting to see if maybe he had seen or heard from them before they took off.

"Pandria, come in," he motioned to me from the doorway.

"Thank you for seeing me, Sir," I bowed.

"Not at all," please come in.

I sat down upon a hard-wooden chair, across from an expansive desk. "Now, how can I help you?"

"Did Atheara or Lillith come to you this morning and let you know where they were going?" I took the forward approach. One of the many things I learned during my first days of my internship.

"No, I have not. I assumed they were still researching through the notes," he looked up and stared through the window.

"Is something wrong?" I inquired. While he was distracted, I unfocused my gaze and follow the fatras flowing through the room. I recognized Atheara's trail immediately. I knew if I pushed the Governor more about the situation, I would head down the confrontational path. I used all my will not to push him further.

"No, nothing is wrong. This business with the missing members of the Science Group and your Mother have us all on edge," the Governor seemed to force a smile.

"I'm sorry to have bothered you. Thank you for your time," I dug my nails into the palm of my hand.

"Not at all," the Governor quickly shook my hand and ushered me out of his office.

I hurried back to Father who was supposed to meet me back at the suite.

"Hello!" I called out. My voice echoed against the walls. I looked around the room and found papers shuffled but no sign of Father. "Hello," I called with panic fighting to burst out of my voice.

"Over here," I heard the muffled call of my Father. I breathed inward and headed over to the far right of the room.

"What are you doing?" I demanded a little more harshly than I intended.

"I found these scribbled notes," Father was oblivious to my moment of fear. "Any news on Atheara or Lillith?"

"No. I even asked the Governor. He swears he has not seen them."

Father paused from scanning the notes and looked up at me, "You don't believe him?"

"I don't know," I began to pace. "I know he's holding something back. I can't tell what secret he is keeping. Even if I tried to push him, he would only cover up what he was hiding."

"What if you followed his lines to see the past?" Father looked up over the papers.

"I suspect the Governor's Seer would instantly know. They may be keeping a close eye on us," I chewed on my bottom lip.

"Still thinking about the mysterious woman you spoke to?" Father eyed me carefully.

"I'm sure it's nothing," I tried to convince myself.

Father nodded and then said, "Look at this," Father tapped the paper. I leaned over his shoulder and read the paper, "The genetic mutation of the plant seems to be incomplete, as if a piece of the code is missing. To erase a code in such a manner is confusing to say the least. . .bits of the fauna are returning but. . .testing will conclude. . ."

"It's jumbled."

"Yes but intriguing all the same."

"What do you mean?"

"Think about it Pandria. Try to remember your science lessons in the Academy. Everything has a genetic structure. For a portion of it to disappear is unheard of. We have been trying to rejuvenate the land beyond The Communities ever since we holed ourselves up here. Now we are seeing some progress bits of it seem to be unraveling. Why?"

"You think that's the question Mother and her team were out here to investigate?"

"It sounds like something your Mother would

want to research."

"She does love puzzles," I sighed. "This doesn't give us any clues as to why she has disappeared. I sure hope whatever happened to Mom has not happened to Atheara and Lillith."

"I didn't realize you care so much about me already," Lillith smirked from the door.

"Where have you been?" I demanded.

"Atheara says rest up; we have a big day tomorrow."

"Why?" I tried to put on my best sneer.

"Just wait and see, Little One," I saw Atheara smile at me from behind Lillith's shoulder.

CHAPTER 7: THE OUTER RIDGE

I had a hard time sleeping, even with the herbal mixture I had to drink. I was not soothed to sleep this time. I tossed and turned, thinking of what could possibly have happened to Mother and her team. What if they were in a sunken hole somewhere and couldn't call for help? Maybe the Governor of the 24th Quadrant had them locked up in some cage somewhere. Maybe they were attacked by some monstrous creature which got through the gates. Many more scenarios played out in my head. I was thankful when the sun began to filter through the window of my room.

Lillith hinted at clothing for outdoor adventuring would be more appropriate than our normal Seer garbs. Lilith unceremoniously threw hiking clothes at me, the boots knocking against my cheek bone and landing softly on my bed. I glared at her as she smirked at me, shutting my door. After tying my boots, I slumped down, placing my head in my hands. Taking several deep breaths, I pulled myself to a standing position, ready to try to resolve this mystery once and for all.

The day was murky. The sun was shadowed by the dust clinging in the air. In the Outer Communities dust storms such as these were common, blowing in from The Barrens.

"Morning," I flopped onto a chair.

"Good morning sunshine," Lillith grumbled.

I looked at her, my cheek still stinging from being whacked in the face by the boots. I looked down at the floor. Listening to her snide remarks was not on my agenda for today.

"Are we ready?" Atheara asked in my mind.

"Where's Father?" I inquired.

"Here," he slung his pack over his shoulders.

"Would anyone be so kind as to tell me where we are going?"

"The Outer Ridge," Lillith stated and walked out the door.

"I thought it took months to get a permit to go out there?"

"Normally, yes," Father explained. "This is a special circumstance. They have expedited the paperwork." He handed over his tablet. I saw the electronic papers signed by the Governor.

"Is this what you were up to yesterday?" I looked at Atheara.

"Of course," she smiled at me and followed Lillith out.

I tossed the bag onto my back and walked out. We boarded the train to head back to the main station. There wasn't a large crowd on this train; not many people went to the Outer Ridges. The Outer Ridges are a dry, barely habitable place. The sun burned through the sky, super heating the ground. During the day those who lived in the Outer Ridges spent their time underground in the mines. During the night they took care of their regular chores in the work camps to maintain their living quarters.

Trees flew by as the train picked up speed. We soon darted through the line of trees separating the last Community to the Outer Ridges. Just out in the distance I saw the slow rise of the Outer Ridges which ended in jagged, rigid teeth. We quickly scuttled out of the car and into the one which would drop us off at a work camp. Atheara remained quiet during our ride to the edge of civilization. She looked thoughtful, scrunching her eyebrows together as she processed one serious thought after another.

"Ever been to the Outer Ridges?" Lillith

plopped down beside me.

"Nope," I let the word jump out of me. There was no reason to try to hide the truth from her. "Have you?"

"Once when I was little. My foster parents took me out here to maintain one of the cars which broke down."

"I didn't realize your foster parents were mechanics."

"Father is a mechanic, Mother a seamstress."

"And your real parents?" I asked before I could stop myself. I stared Lillith down, knowing I wanted to know the answer to the question.

I thought she was going to refuse to respond to me. Lillith said, "Father was the Governor of The City and Mother was an ambassador in the Quadrant."

"So, you probably inherited the genes to become a potential."

"It happens," Lillith dismissed the observation.

"Please tell me you aren't one of those who praise the gift of the Seers."

"No," I firmly stated.

She eyed me quietly. After a while she got up,

leaving me to alone. The train came to a full stop. We exited the train. The work camp was dusty and filled with tents made of white canvass. Cooking fires were arranged in a semi-circle in the middle of all the tents. I saw cots in each one of the tents as we walked by. The sun was already causing me to perspire out in the dry heat.

"Morning," an elderly man shook Father's hand. "Papers please."

Father dug his tablet out of his bag and flicked it on. He must have left the screen of our papers on the main screen because he didn't have to go searching through any of his multitude of files.

"Name is Kempton though some call me Kemp," he motioned for us to follow him. "This is our camp. You are welcome to stay. Most Community members don't have the stomach for it."

"I'm sure we will be just fine."

"If you consider roasting alive fine," Lillith growled.

"Shh," I tried to tamper down her blunt behavior.

"No worries Potential," Kemp turned towards me. "We are used to such ill feelings around here."

He took us to the last two tents at the camp.

"These are our guest tents. We rarely ever use them. Expect dust lining everything," he pulled the flap open. "You ladies can stay in here and you, Sir, can stay in the tent next door. We eat after dusk. You are welcome to join us." Kemp walked away from us.

"Not much on helping us, is he?" Lillith mocked.

"Mining is a busy life. As you can see, it gets rough," Father stared at Kemp's back as he walked out of our line of sight.

"If we are going to the mines we better do so quickly before the sun is directly overhead. If we wait too long, we will either be stuck sitting in the tents or pass out from heat exhaustion."

"Where to?" I asked Atheara.

"Mines. Workers had stated he saw your Mother's group nearby."

Instead of settling into our new home we marched off towards the mines. The land was rough, devoid of most vegetation and other natural wildlife. I saw a few sprigs of grass trying desperately to grow out here in the Outer Ridges. In the skyline I saw encircling us the rock face which gave this area its name. There were broken spots in the skyline where you can see past the Outer Ridges to the smooth wall which protected us from The Barrens. Most of the rock formations looked jagged and uninviting.

We didn't pass anyone as we walked to the first of the mines in the lower part of the Ridges. No one would be foolhardy enough to come out here in the daylight. The sun's heat weighed heavily upon my brow, sweat dripping down my neck as we finally approached the shadow of the first ridge.

"Here we are," Father reached into his pack pulling out a flashlight.

"Here we are," I parroted.

"Come in, then," an inpatient gentleman waved at us from the shadow of the mine entrance. We walked forward passing through iron gates which stood open. "Why you want to stay out in the sun is beyond me."

He silently walked us down a tunnel to the far left. Just beyond I could make out a faint glow of light spill out from a doorway built into the tunnel. "Here you are mam," the gentleman spoke to another person in the room. He gave us a scrutinizing look then padded off back down the tunnel.

"Welcome," a weathered woman stood up from behind an oak desk. "Please come in. My name is Jacobe and the gentleman who just left is Merriwether."

"Nice to meet you," I shook her hand.

"The rest of you must be Potential Lillith, Master Atheara, and Mr. Arturas," she shook each of their hands.

"I am told you are here to find the missing Science Group."

"Yes," Father replied. "My wife, Pandria's Mother," he motioned to me, "Was amongst them."

"Science groups have been coming out here for years.

"Do you know why?" Father inquired.

"I don't ask questions. We have many things to do here in the mines."

"Do you have a guess?" I asked hopefully.

"Well, I assume they are checking on the regrowth progress along the line of the Outer Ridges."

I bit back my retort. The look in her eyes betrayed her. She knew more and wasn't going to share whatever it was she was holding back. I looked over at Lillith and saw a line crease her forehead. I realized this woman was fighting Lillith's gift. Normal people wouldn't be able to hold back the full truth. I felt the urge to blurt out this revelation. I managed to keep it to myself. My Father, on the other hand, was not so fortunate.

"You're not telling us the truth," he demanded.

"Look, Mr. Arturas, I realize you and your daughter are reasonably upset over this ordeal. I know I would be. My focus is on the mines, not scientist coming back and forth."

Lillith gazed intently at Jacobe, "You are not allowed to speak to us about this, are you?"

Jacobe stared at Lillith for a minute before answering, "If there is anything more I can help you with please let me know," she gestured towards the door.

"Enough, Lillith, Pandria, let's go," Atheara's voice clearly stated in our minds.

Father began to protest. I put a hand on his shoulder and shook my head slightly towards Atheara. He gritted his teeth then marched out the door.

"What is it, Atheara?" I asked her as we entered the main tunnel away from the very unhelpful Jacobe.

"You know as much as I there is something not right about her," she pointedly looked at Lillith.

"She should have told us the truth. She fought Lillith's gift."

Father looked back and forth. I just nodded towards the door, letting him know I would fill him in later about what we had discussed with Atheara mentally. Some things were best left unsaid when more ears weren't listening. Merriwether was back, motioning for us to enter one of the cars. I hadn't heard any bell or anything. I wondered how he knew we were ready to go.

"I'm going to take you to where they were last seen," he stated.

"They were in the mines?" I asked as the car began to pull away from the main tunnel.

"No. We often use the mines to travel to the different parts of the Outer Ridges."

We were unable to ask questions after the car started moving, the wind roaring in our ears. At times, the tunnels we zipped through were hot while others were ice cold. Many hours later we came to a stop, sunlight filtering through an opening in the tunnel we just stopped in.

"Here we are tunnel 17, Outer Ridge Meadows."

We clambered out of the tunnel car, feeling a little wobbly on our legs.

"I wish there were another way to travel through these confounded tunnels," Atheara complained.

Lillith simply shook her head in agreement, her face pure white.

Father, on the other hand, looked like he had just been on a simple train ride to The City. "They were studying The Meadow?" he inquired.

"Yes. Feel free to look around. The sun is dipping below the ridge line so you shouldn't fear being burned."

Father nodded and walked out. A field was a nice way of putting it. I imagined at one point there must have been beautiful flowers and lush vegetation. The only signs of those now were a scrap of grass or a bit of weed poking up through the ashen mud lining the oval impression between bits of the Ridges stabbing the sky. Parts were muddy, looking more like tar than ground. Father treaded carefully, poking around the edge of the meadow.

"Stay close to the outside of The Meadow. Heaven knows what the consistency the ground is like if you venture to the center."

Lillith sighed loudly and began to search the opposite side of Father. Atheara and I followed in their wake. I bent down a couple of times, eyeing the vegetation carefully. After an hour of searching Atheara asked me, "Should we sit at the base of the tunnel and see if we can follow the fatras?"

I nodded to her and relayed our plan to Father. "I think that's a good idea."

"Sit quietly, Pandria. Let the sunlight go and focus on the golden threads which crisscross out here."

I combined my thoughts with hers, the golden fatras interlacing all through the field. Mother had definitely been here. I recognized the aura twinge around several of the fatras. Her color was very distinct, the color of a deep amber. I could feel Lillith's presence. She had joined in our search. Her presence was foreign, a dark rose color with an orange tinge within it. Even with just her mentally with us I felt the truth of the area enhanced the fatras even more. They became clearer, more certain. Even with the three of us working together the fatras began to unravel just beyond the Outer Ridges. Atheara pulled us quickly back.

Father rushed to my side, "Pandria, are you alright?"

I was breathing hard, sweat beading upon my arms and sliding down my back. Every time I came across the fatras disappearing I felt as if I were suffocating. "Yes Father, I am okay," I nodded.

Lillith looked whiter than when we got out of the train car. "You okay?" I looked at her.

"Yes," she was trying to catch her breath.

"Atheara?" I asked in my mind.

"I'm okay Little One," she smiled weakly at me.

"Father," I looked up at him. "She was here. We aren't sure where they went."

"Merriwether, do you know what they were doing here?" he asked.

Merriwether had been sitting idly by the car. When Father asked his question, he got up and wandered over to us, "They were studying the growth rate," he rattled. "As you can see, there isn't much progress. I think one of them was taking samples back to the lab."

"That's all they were doing?" Father looked up at him. I knew what he was thinking. If the lady Jacobe was lying to us, then this man was probably lying to us as well.

Merriwether replied briskly, "Yes Sir."

I looked at Atheara and asked her in my mind, "Do you think he is able to lie, too?"

Atheara stared at Lillith then back at me, "No, she thinks he isn't able to resist the urge to tell the truth."

"Thank you, Merriwether," I stood up with the help of Father. "We should probably head back.

By the time we get back it will be late."

"Very well Miss."

We loaded into the car and flew back down the tunnel. When we reached the tunnel entrance the last rays of light were floating behind the Outer Ridges. We walked out of the tunnel. I breathed deeply. The fresh air was more preferable to the stuffiness of the tunnels. I noticed Merriwether was not walking to the work camp with us.

"You're not joining us?"

"No, Mam, I must leave you here. I have work to finish before retiring for the night." I felt a pang of guilt from keeping him from his work.

"Thank you again," Father tried to put on his best smile.

Without another word Merriwether turned his back to us and walked back into the tunnel.

"Such abrupt people," Lillith growled. She then walked a quick pace towards the camp.

I shook my head and followed. "What do you think Mother's group found looking in the field?" I asked Father.

"Well, the ground is not conducive to growing plant life," he shrugged.

"Do you think she thinks of us?" I grabbed his hand.

Father smiled at me, "Why wouldn't she?"

There were many men and women at the camp. Fires crackled and the last of the sun slipped behind the Ridges. I smelled pork and heard fat sizzling over the fire. My stomach grumbled. I wasn't hungry until the moment I smelled food.

"I see you made it through the first day," Kemp heaped beans and pork upon plates and passed them to us. "Didn't think Community folks would last through a whole day but here you are."

"Yes, funny that," Lillith hissed.

"Don't mind her," I watched Lillith storm away with her plate of food.

"Not much on the truth, is she?" he asked.

I suppressed a giggle. "More than you think."

Father rolled his eyes and found a log to sit on. We ate in silence while some workers started singing a folk song. I didn't recognize the tune and listened carefully.

"To the trails we walk, ever in the dark. The sun so bright it burns away light. We work all day; we live by the night. Welcome weary travelers to the end of life."

Their voices broke off from their unison singing, harmonizing with each other. I thought of their words with worried wonderment. The Ridges were often described as the end of any chance of civilization. Beyond the land was unforgiving and desolate. We had left it ravaged by war. They said nothing could survive beyond the jagged tooth mountains. Most scientists who ventured beyond the Outer Ridges did not return. Even if one survived their skin was blistered beyond belief. The further you went to the edge of the Outer Ridges the more the sun beat through the atmosphere, searing everything within its reach. The wars had destroyed parts of our atmosphere. We were lucky to have what we did in The Communities.

I washed my dishes and stood up, "Good night," I yawned and stretched. Atheara had left earlier to the tent we were given for the duration of our stay here.

"Night Pandria," Father smiled at me.

I fell onto the cot Kempton had provided. I woke the next morning fully clothed in the clothes I had on the day before. The sun was just cresting the Outer Ridges. Atheara was already up, going through her morning meditation before starting the day. I waited until she spoke to me.

"Good morning, Little One. How did you sleep?"

"My eyes were closed," I stiffly replied. "I still feel tired."

"I know what you mean."

I quickly changed. The air was cold as I was dressing. Atheara tossed a nutrient bar to me. I gobbled it down quickly. We found Father outside his tent along with Lillith.

"Where do we go from here?" she asked.

"We need to go back into the tunnels," Atheara stated. I think there are other tunnels they went down to reach some of the other crevices in the Outer Ridges."

I explained Atheara's thoughts to Father. "Yes, I think you may be right. I read in their notes they were interested in the southern region as well. We should start there."

"You think Merriwether would be willing to take us there?" I frowned.

"Will, they have been amendable so far."

"Let's not get our hopes up," Lillith scowled and headed towards the tunnels. "I hate those infernal cars."

As we entered the tunnels, I saw Merriwether waiting there to greet us. "Good morning folks." He tipped his hat to us.

"Good morning," I yawned.

He laughed at me, "Not a morning person?"

"No," I shook my head.

"Where to?" he looked at Dad.

"Southern section if you please."

He scratched his beard, "I'm not sure going to the southern area is a good idea."

"Why?" Father asked.

"The atmosphere there isn't as stable as the eastern side. I will take you there if you insist."

"Please," I looked at him.

He scrutinized my anxious face. For a brief second, I saw it soften. He gruffly said, "Hop in, I warned you."

The trip took a little longer. We wound left then right, slowly making our way south. The stench here was stronger, more sulfur than the mildew smell of the other tunnels. Just when I thought I was going to lose my breakfast the wheels squeaked to a sudden halt. Lillith looked like she was going to pass out.

"Here we are," he said. "I will wait here. I brought some work. I need to check some of the tunnels. I will meet you back here in about four hours."

"Thank you," Father nodded.

"Here," Atheara pointed to the exit of the tunnel. The heat could be seen radiating off the moisture in the rocks.

We couldn't exit the tunnels. The sun was searing just at the entrance. We had to hide within the shadows.

"No good," Father stood behind me. "One step out there and we will likely end up with second degree burns."

"I think the girls and I need to look in a different way," Atheara sat cross legged on the hard ground. Father nodded. He went off down a tunnel to take a look around, searching in his own way.

Lillith and I sat on either side of Atheara, letting ourselves delve into the world of the fatras. I felt Lillith's strange presence again mixed with the familiar companionship of Atheara.

"There," I heard Lillith whisper. The fatras we had seen before were here as well.

Mother's scientist group had gone out in this

area. I had the distinct feeling they came here at night. They wandered through the sand stones which were piled throughout the clearing. They dug down into the dirt, searching for weeds which did not exist up here. Mother's companions hesitated, checking into a stone structure which looked broken. They were scrapping pieces of the sandstone into vials. They placed them in canvas bags which held remnants of plant life they had found from the field we were at yesterday. They climbed higher and higher, trying to reach a vantage point to look out over the entire Outer Ridges. As we reached the height of the tallest spike of the Outer Edge the lines of the fatras burned away with the sun. The three of us screamed out in pain. I felt my eyes tear, stinging as they streamed down my face.

Father and Merriwether were both by our sides. We must have been searching longer than I thought. Looking into the fatras took time.

"Atheara," I heard my Dad gasp. I looked up and noticed her face was slightly redder than normal.

I grasped her hand and held it tightly, "Atheara, you okay?"

"Little One," I heard her voice weakly in mind. She did not open her eyes.

"Quickly, get her into the car," Father instructed to Merriwether. Together they lifted her up and gently placed her in the car. "Pandria, Lillith, hop in quickly. We must get her help." Lillith had tears streaming down her face. She hastily wiped them away, cradling Atheara's head. Up to this point I hadn't seen Lillith show any affinity to anyone. Perhaps there was a softer side to her. With a lurch the car sped through the tunnels, the wind whistling in our ears.

CHAPTER 8: HERBALIST

There was no herbologist out here in the Outer Ridges. Most workers knew how to address minor injuries or set major physical wounds until they could get the injured to an herbologist. The closest one was in Quadrant 24, just a mile from the Political House where we had stayed.

Kemp helped Father load Atheara onto the train, instructing the driver to contact the herbologist on the way. He looked intently at the group of us, our bags thrown haphazardly on various seats. Lillith still held Atheara's head in her lap.

"Hang on Atheara," tears seeped from my eyes. Lillith held her hand, squeezing it at different intervals to assure Atheara was still alive. Her breathing was ragged and jarring. She did not speak to either of us. Her eyes remained closed. What felt like a short distance coming out took a lifetime to get back. When the train finally stopped in front of the Herbalist Building, I jumped up and ran to the door. The plaque in front read Evert. I pounded on the hard wood with both of my hands.

"Coming, coming," I heard the muffled reply of a woman's voice.

"Oh my!" she exclaimed as Father carried Atheara in her arms. "Potential," she looked at me. "Quickly tell me what's happened."

"We were in the Outer Ridges, following the fatras of a lost science group," I ignored her incorrect usage of the word potential. "When we reached the boundary between the Ridges and The Barrens the sun seemed to sear the fatras away. I think Atheara was too far ahead of us. She didn't have our support when we came up against it," my hands shook as I tried to soothe Atheara's graying hair away from her wrinkled face.

"Moonlace, bittersweet, mint, and dartsmeld," she pointed towards the shelf in the back room. Lillith darted to the back room to grab the ingredients Evert listed off. Father placed Atheara on a sterile, wooden table, laying her head upon a pillow which was positioned at one end of it.

Lillith came back and placed the vials on a counter near the table. Evert came back with a bottle of thick grayish liquid and began measuring bits of the vials into it. "Will she be all right?"

Lillith gazed intently at Evert.

Evert glanced up at Lillith and before she could stop herself said, "I've never seen this before. I have no idea." She looked back up at Lillith, alarmed.

"Never mind," Lillith grumbled.

Although Evert was disturbed by her own reaction to Lillith she worked in earnest. After mixing ingredients carefully together she smoothed some of the mixture on Atheara's cheeks. Evert examined Atheara's pulse and other vitals. After a thorough examination she went into the back room and pulled out a couple of other herbs and medicines I didn't recognize. She pulled a tube from a drawer and a bag. Evert hung the bag next to Atheara. In the bag she injected some of the medicine and carefully slid a needled tube into her arm. After messaging the bag, the liquid began to drip into her veins. I heard a sigh of relief escape Atheara's lips. I could sense Atheara going into a deep sleep.

"What did you give her?" I looked up at Evert.

"A pain-relieving sedative. The sedative will help her sleep and let her body heal."

"What's happened to her?"

Evert looked at Lillith, a frown etched into her face. "As I've already stated, I've never seen this before. I believe she will recover. I will keep a close eye on her the next 48 hours to make sure she will be alright," she gave my shoulder a squeeze. Evert looked up at Father, "You might want to contact the Seer Council to let them know what happened. If Atheara takes a turn for the worse, they may need to send someone with more skill out to help her," she looked frustrated and glared at Lillith. Lillith scowled back and stomped off into the entryway of the Herbalist Building.

"Happens to everyone," I responded to Evert before she could ask any questions. I followed Lillith out to the entryway.

Father followed me out, "Let's go back to the Political House. I will use their phone to call the Great Seer Council."

I shook my head, "I want to stay with Atheara. I don't want to leave her here by herself."

"I would stay but if I do, I'm afraid Evert will have a nervous breakdown. She can't handle my 'gift'," she stormed out of the door.

Father looked after her, a puzzled look on his face. "Okay, stay out of trouble," he kissed the top of my head.

I walked back into the Infirmary Room where Atheara lay. Evert was in a side room, staring at a screen. I glanced at the screen and saw it had

Atheara's vitals. I pulled a chair over to the table, placing my small hand over Atheara's hand.

A few minutes later Trice, Seer Ambassador at the Political House, came barging into the room. She rushed to the opposite side of the table from me, checking her vitals and carefully examining her outer wounds.

"Trice," Evert was trying to keep her temper in check. "I have administered a burn salve and have her on an IV of a sedative painkiller. Unless you have seen this type of thing before I'm not sure what else we can do."

Trice looked at Evert and took a deep breath. "No, none of the Masters have seen this type of thing before. They wanted me to check on her and report back to them."

"Very well," Evert responded in crisp tones.

Trice stood still, following the fatras around Atheara. After moments in silence, she began poking and prodding Atheara, checking her pulse and listening to her breathing. As she did so she asked me, "Where were you when this happened?"

"We were in the southern section of the Outer Ridges."

"What were you doing when this happened?"

"We were following the fatras of the science group. The fatras ended at the boundary of the Outer Ridges. The Fate Lines felt like they were being burned away by the sun."

Trice looked up when I said this and stared intently at me, "Neither you nor Lillith were affected by this?"

"I think Atheara managed to get ahead of us. We were trying to work together just in case there were any problems."

"What problems?" she came around the table. "Were you expecting problems?" her voice sounded accusing.

"Enough Trice," Evert came out from her room. "If you are going to accuse Pandria of anything, or Atheara for that matter, please do so outside the room. I don't want my patient to feel the stress. She's already gone through enough for today."

I noticed Atheara was breathing harder. I realized what Evert said was true. She must have sensed the tension in the room. I motioned for Trice to follow me out to the entryway. "Atheara noticed the fatras seem to be disappearing. She was fearful of what would happen if one of us tried to follow them alone out here. She had us work together in hopes this would alleviate any chance of danger. I'm certain she spoke to the

Seer Council about this," I crossed my arms.

Trice seemed to be assessing me then sighed, "They said as much. I had to be certain."

"What do you mean certain? Has there been some type of threat issued against the Seers?"

"No. They seemed concerned about some external force working against the peace we have worked hard to maintain. Some think it may be possible someone is working to cause war again."

"It's not us," I shouted.

"Pandria!" Evert's voice warned from the Infirmary Room.

"Sorry," I whispered. I began to count backwards from 10 and focused on regulating my breathing.

Trice had taken a step towards me and placed a gentle hand on my arm, "I believe you, Pandria. They wanted me to be certain."

I mutely nodded.

She turned towards the door then looked back at me, "If it helps, I think Evert is doing everything possible to help Atheara. She will be alright. It's hard to tell, her fatras are fuzzy and uncertain."

"Is that even possible?" I looked up, worried.

"At times in our history this has happened."

"Rare?"

"Rare," she agreed. With this last word Trice was out of the door, the night air streaming in.

I looked back to the Infirmary Room and called out, "I am going to get some air. I will be back soon." I heard the muffled acknowledgement from Evert as I walked out the door. The stars shone brightly in the sky, the moon only a sliver tonight. Directly across from the Herbalist Building was an herb garden, wooden benches scattered throughout. I sat down at the very center of the garden, crossing my legs close to me.

I let the smell of mint leaves and lavender wash over me. Breathing in deeply I inhaled their calming scents. I forced myself to slow my breathing, in and out. I entered the meditative state Atheara had taught me. I let my mind clear, leaving behind even the fatras. Any time a worried thought entered my mind I forced the negative energy out. I focused solely on the fatras as I opened my eyes and saw the golden threads network in front of me. My own fatras flowed out, three lines spreading before me. The left was crystal clear, the right burned with a fire glow, and straight ahead was a hazy gray. I let these lines go and followed other lines, not seeing anything familiar besides the commonality of the golden thread in the middle. Stopping at the Political House I picked up the familiar aura of my Mother. I watched, the lines crossing all around the 24th Quadrant out to the Outer Ridges. I pulled my sights back in, finding it a little difficult to pull back to where I was sitting. Time was slowing. I let my mind clear again, focusing on the scents and sounds around me. I opened my eyes and went back in the Herbology building.

I felt the worry still. The meditation made it manageable, less panic and more concern filled me. I held Atheara's hand once again and whispered before falling asleep in my chair, "What happened, Atheara?"

Light filtered through dusty glass in the room. My hair was sticking to my hand as I had my head upon it. Atheara was still breathing deeply. Evert was checking her vitals again, a tablet in her hand as she jotted down notes.

"How is she?" my voice croaked.

"Better than you at the moment," she eyed me critically. "You need to go eat, rest properly, or you will be no help to Atheara."

Lillith came in at this moment. Evert looked up with dismay written all over her face. I suppressed a smirk and looked up at Lillith. "Perfect timing."

"Always," she smiled at me. "Go, I will watch her."

I stretched and headed towards the door. "Was there any more news from the Temple?"

"No."

"Of course not," I grumbled. Instead of hopping onto a train I walked back to the Political House which bustled with senators, secretaries, and other official looking people. Our adventure to the Outer Ridges had stirred up a heap of activity. After confirming we were using the same rooms we had before, I found Father in our common area. He was looking disheveled.

"How is she?"

"Evert says she is healing. Anything from the Temple?"

"No, Trice reported to them last night and they were content with whatever she told them."

"Then why is the house full?"

"The government is nervous and suspicious. Get some sleep, you look like you could use a good meal and some rest."

"Suspicious about what?" I crossed my arms.

"To bed," Father commanded. I was briefly reminded of when I was five years old, not wanting to go to bed.

"Fine, fine," I didn't want to argue with him. I grabbed a breakfast bar from the cupboard in the kitchen and headed to my room. The silence was a much welcome sound to the hustle and bustle of the rest of the house. Sleep came fast and was devoid of dreams.

A short time later Lillith was shaking my arm. "Pandria," she sounded frustrated.

"Yea, yea. I'm awake."

"Good, Atheara is asking for you."

This jolted me awake. I sat straight up almost knocking Lillith over.

"You might want to take a shower first," Lillith pinched her nose.

"Nice," I rolled my eyes. "Wait, who's with her right now?"

"Your Father is with her. Don't look so worried."

I widely yawned and rolled out of bed. She sauntered off. I heard her door click shut. I pulled out some clothes and padded to the bathroom. The shower was small, and the water barely trickled out. After dressing in a fresh set of clothes, I stopped by the kitchen and grabbed another breakfast bar. I knew Atheara wouldn't approve. I didn't want to waste any more time. The Political House was quiet even with the increase in personnel. I exited without being stopped by anyone. I reached the herbologist in a short amount of time. Father was sitting beside Atheara, his chair kicked back. As I walked in, he thunked down to the floor.

"Good morning sleepy," Father chuckled and ruffled my hair.

"Looks like night to me," I muttered.

"Little One," Atheara's voice was weak with exhaustion.

"Are you okay?" I asked her.

"Yes, thank you," she reached her hand out to me. I took it.

Evert came bustling out, looking hassled. "Her vitals are stronger. Her cheeks are healing nicely. She still needs to stay here for observation."

"She's trying to leave, isn't she?" I scowled at Atheara.

"You try getting comfortable on a wooden table," Atheara grumbled in my head.

"Is there a bed we can move her to?" I asked Evert instead.

"Yes, the recovery rooms are this way," she

motioned to the left.

"Is it safe to move her?" Father stood up.

"Yes. We will need to keep her IV in. If you can carry her, we can move her to the recovery room without any problems," Evert moved to the table. She tapped on the bag then lifted it off its hook.

Father lifted Atheara into his arms, "My hero," Atheara's voice laughed in my head.

"Be nice," I said aloud.

Father lifted an eyebrow at me but didn't ask. He placed her on a bed close to one of the glass windows. "Better?" he asked.

"A little, yes," she said.

"She said yes," I told Father.

Evert placed the bag on a hook next to the bed. "Paraphraser," Atheara accused me.

"Complainer," I retorted in my head.

"You guys don't need to hover over me," her voice began to fade.

"Sleep," I told her as I pulled a chair next to the bed. Evert made some more notes on her tablet then shuffled off to her office. There were no other patients in the recovery room.

"Pandria," Father sat beside me. "Do you know

what caused this?"

"I'm not sure," I looked thoughtfully at him. "Like I told Trice, we were following the fatras. Once we got to the boundary of the Outer Ridges the fatras burned away. I think Atheara was burned, too," I whispered.

"I'm glad you were not hurt," he squeezed my hand. I squeezed his hand back.

"I'm sorry we haven't gotten any closer to finding Mother," I could feel hot tears on my face.

"We will find her."

I nodded, wanting to believe him.

"The Governor came here earlier today. He said he has sent an envoy out to the mines to speak to the workers. He wants to see if they have noticed anything unusual."

"I don't think they are going to be able to find anything."

"I agree. I think he feels the need to do something to look good in the eyes of the Seer Council. One of theirs has been hurt. They are going to want some answers."

"They said they already tried to find the missing group and came up empty. That's why we are here," I rubbed my temples.

"Yes, with the injury of Atheara they felt like they needed to look more productive."

"All about looks," I sighed.

"Pandria, be careful of what you say."

"Sorry Father."

"You're an Ambassador out here, even if you haven't finished your internship," he scolded.

"You sound like Atheara," I smiled.

"Smart woman," he chuckled.

"Do you think Mother is okay?" I looked up hopefully at him.

"What do you think?" he looked directly at me.

"I want to think she is," I truthfully stated.

"Then she is," he smiled.

I admired his unfailing belief. We sat quietly, both lost in our own thoughts. The moon shone high through the window when Lillith came in.

"The envoy has come back with nothing," Lillith whispered. "Is she doing better?"

"Yes," I whispered. Father was snoring lightly in his chair.

"Did she say anything about what happened?"

"No. She just asked to be moved to a more comfortable place."

"That's something," Lillith sat down on the other side of me.

"Have you spoken to Trice?"

"Not helpful that one."

"She seemed like she wanted to be helpful," I defended her.

"Wanting and being are two different verbs," Lillith criticized.

"Not much on cheerfulness, are you?" I spat back.

Father's snores stuttered and we both looked at him, waiting for his snoring to return. When he returned to a smoother cadence of sleep I whispered, "Let's agree on one thing."

"Just one?"

"We both care about Atheara and what's going on here. They are both connected. It's up to us to figure this out."

"I suppose I will count all of those things as one," Lillith conceded. "All right," she reached out her hand.

"Enough of the cynical attitude?" I held out

my own hand.

"How about just sarcastic?"

I shook her hand, "Deal. I don't really blame you."

"Blame me for what?"

"The cynicism."

"How do you figure?"

"Well, I'm sure it gets annoying to have people blurting out their deep, dark truths all the time."

"Probably just as annoying as always seeing fatras wherever you go. Do you mistake them for something you might trip over?" she said with a hint of satire in her voice.

"Only when I am very sleepy," I laughed.

"What has Trice said?" I tried again.

I saw Lillith grit her teeth and then respond, "She said it was a freak accident. Somehow the radiation in the area must have penetrated our sight therefore burning Atheara. As if Atheara would be careless."

"Really? Freak accident? That's all they are willing to call it?"

"Do you know if Atheara has spoken to the Council about the fatras?"

"She told me she had. I'm not sure what she has told them. Or what they have told her."

"Everyone seems to know there is a problem and not willing to do anything about it."

"What about that woman who approached us? Have you seen her since we returned?"

"No, you?"

"No."

"A lot of questions with no answers. We should be able to foresee the future."

"We see possible outcomes, not causation or the end solution to those outcomes."

"Fair enough," she sat back in her chair. "What if we are reading the fatras incorrectly?"

"I'm not sure I follow?"

"Well, I was actually sent on this assignment because I kept questioning the Masters about how we interpret the fatras. It's a legitimate question. They felt I was being a pest. I needed to get away from the Centre for a while. What if what we think is the correct path is indeed not?"

"My experience has been if I follow the blazing fatras line bad things happen."

"Yes, those are one of the lines. Yet, who is to

say it is the wrong path to take?"

"What? Are we are supposed to endure great amounts of pain? If it weren't for the first Seer our society would still be in war."

"Perhaps," Lillith sat up again. "Or perhaps our perception of the possible outcome is incorrect. Just something we want to think."

"I don't know," I pondered her response. "Our society has been at peace for a long time because of our guidance."

"And now strange and dark things are happening."

I thought about her side of the argument. I knew peace was essential to the continued existence of The Communities. Now the fatras were disappearing. Following them caused pain for the Seers who were supposed to read them. Science told us for every action there was an opposite and equal reaction.

We sat, each pondering this argument. I knew Lillith had valid points. To be a Seer meant we were given a gift. A gift we should use. I couldn't see why we would have such a power and not use it. Father stood up and yawned.

"Not all of us were able to sleep through the day. I'm calling it a night, ladies."

"Night Dad."

"You girls should also get some rest," Atheara's voice weakly entered our minds. I began to protest. She said, "I am out of danger, go."

I nodded and stood up at the same time as Lillith.

As our footfalls crunched on the gravel trail leading back to the Political House. Lillith stated, "I wonder what the woman at the mines is hiding."

"I'm not even sure how she was able to hide anything."

"I don't know either. Most people barely resist the urge to spill out their deep dark truths. She acted as if hiding secrets was second nature to her."

Father was ahead of us and therefore wasn't paying attention to our conversation. "There was something very peculiar about her."

The Political House was silent, almost eerily so. Trice was sitting in her office as we passed.

"How is Atheara doing tonight?"

"Better," Father stopped in front of us. "She's awake at least."

"That's great," Trice looked relieved. "The Seer

Council will be pleased to hear this news."

"Do you have everything you need here? I know you all left the mines quickly," Trice smiled at Father.

"We're fine, thank you," Father bowed. "I think we are going to call it a night."

"Good night," I waved to Trice as we continued on to the rooms.

Dinner was a brief affair. All of us were too tired to put much care or effort into the food. We had a simple soup Father whipped up. Without another word we all wandered to bed.

At night, the dreams came back. Mother was with her science group near the southern Outer Ridge area. The small area just outside the tunnel was filled with a thick curling smoke, bright orange flames flickered. The science group was unaware of these flames as they exited the tunnel out into the inferno.

"Stop!" I tried to shout at them. The words were stuck in my throat as I inhaled the suffocating smoke, choking on its acrid smell.

I reached out to grab Mother's arm. All I ended up grabbing was a flame which seared my hand. I screamed in pain and tightly held it against my chest.

"Pandria!" I heard my name called. Mother turned around and looked at me, eyes wide with fright.

"Pandria!" an urgent voice shook me out of my slumber.

Lillith was shaking me, dodging my arms as they flailed about. I sat up quickly, sweat pouring down my arms. Tremors shook my body. I gripped the edges of the bed trying to slow my heart rate by taking deep breaths.

"Are you okay?" Lillith looked at me with deep concern.

"Yes," I gasped. I felt as if the smoke were still trapped in my lungs. "Just a dream," I tried to convince myself.

"About your Mother again?"

"Yes." I had learned if I kept my answers short, I wouldn't feel the need to blurt out what I was really thinking around Lillith.

"Pandria, it's okay. Tell me what happened please," Lillith sat down at the edge of my bed.

I hesitated and stared at my hands. On one hand it would be nice to share my nightmare with someone, like pulling a thorn out of your finger. However, Lilith and I were not close to friends. We had only just found a middle ground so we could get along. She looked intently at me. I saw something I had missed before in her eyes; sincerity. "The southern part of the Outer Ridges was on fire. Mother and the other scientists had no idea what they were walking into. I tried to warn them, shout at them. I couldn't because of all the smoke. Mother turned and looked at me this time."

"Sounds terrifying," Lillith sounded genuinely concerned.

I looked around and realized Father had not come running in. I think Lillith saw my look of confusion. She said, "I was having trouble sleeping, too. I heard you flinging around when I got up to get some water."

I slipped out of bed and slipped on some shoes.

"Where are you going?" Lillith looked confused.

"I think we both need to take the advice of Atheara and do some meditation in the garden."

"I really can't argue with that," Lillith frowned as if she were really disappointed she couldn't argue against me.

The night air washed over us, clearing my mind as I hoped it would. We sat cross legged on a wooden bench. I took in the sounds of the night as I had before forcing my mind to clear of all thought. It took longer than before, with the dream still fresh in my mind. Lillith got up before I did, nodded to me, and then went back inside. I watched a shooting star streak across the sky. I returned indoors. As I laid in bed, I felt the heat of the dream burn against my arms. I held fast onto the cool night air washing over, sending me into an uneasy sleep.

The next day shone bright through the slit of the window. Father and Lillith had already gone to the herbologist. I headed out the door to join them.

CHAPTER 9:
THE CITY

"Governor Cooley, Atheara says she appreciates your concern. She feels she is able to continue the search for Mrs. Arturas and her colleagues Hill and Gibson," Lillith had her arms crossed, sternly talking to the Governor.

I took a deep breath before entering, "What's going on?"

"The Governor wants to send us back to the Centre," Lillith glared.

"Lillith, enough," Atheara spoke to the both of us. "Little One, tell the Governor we will comply with the Council's request to return. I know they only want to be certain I am completely better before continuing our search."

"Are you sure, Atheara?" Lillith asked.

"Yes."

I turned to Governor Cooley and avoided looking at my Father, "Atheara says we will comply with the Council's request so they can be certain of her recovery." I swallowed down the large lump building in my throat. I wasn't angry with Atheara. I was still concerned about her. I wasn't willing to stop the search for Mother either. I bit down on my lip to subside the war inside my heart.

"Very good," Cooley bowed. "The Council wanted me to let you know your search will not end. They simply need to make sure Atheara will be okay. You will all stay in the Centre, including Mr. Arturas. When Atheara is ready you may all continue your search."

"What will we do while we are waiting?" Lillith let anger seep into her words.

"They will have tasks for you to check into Lillith and Pandria. Mr. Arturas, you may check in with your job as I'm sure they have something for you to work on during this break."

No one spoke until the Governor left the room. "What did that mean, break?" Lillith slammed the door.

"Presumably, a period of time we won't be looking for Mother," I walked over to Atheara. "How are you feeling?" The frustration I was feeling had evaporated when I looked at the paleness of Atheara.

"Better," Atheara pulled herself up further on

her pillow. "I think we will be leaving tonight."

"Do you find Governor Cooley's behavior strange?" I smoothed down the blankets on her bed.

"A little. It's not like the Council to want to send a recovering patient back to the Centre with such urgency. If I was getting worse, I would understand. I am healing quickly."

"What is it, Pandria?" Father came up behind me. I saw Lillith twirling her hair over by the window; a very girly thing for her to do.

"I don't know, something just doesn't feel right. I understand their concern about Atheara. However, she's healing at a rapid rate. They seem to be frantic to get us back to the Centre."

"Maybe they just want to be careful. There's no harm in being too careful," he gave me a hug. I could tell he was agitated by this delay. Father was trying to be as supportive as he could.

"I hope you're right," Lillith turned to face us. "Better go pack up before they shove us onto the train without our stuff." She haughtily opened the door. I watched her disappear before looking up at Father.

"You're probably right. They may just want to be sure Atheara is healing quickly since we are unsure what caused her to be ill in the first place," I chewed on my lower lip. "Still, I think there's more going on here than they are telling us."

"We should keep our eyes and ears open," he started to head back to gather his stuff. He paused and turned back around, "There is such a thing as overcautious, though."

I smiled back at Dad. He was a perpetual optimist of people. He turned back around and walked out towards the Political House.

Later in the morning I pulled my pack onto my back and held Atheara's bag in my other hand. I wasn't keen on her traveling so soon after being burned the way she was by the disappearing fatras. I insisted on 'over' helping her which began to grate on Atheara's nerves. I let her rant about how capable she was in helping herself. I promptly ignored her protests. They had her in a wheelchair, insisting she shouldn't put stress upon her body yet until they were certain she would be fine. Herbalist Evert was riding to the Centre with us, her medical bag packed and ready to go. The train pulled up and silently pulled to a stop in front of us. When it came to a full stop Herbalist Honor and Kenston both stepped out of the train. Honor was from the Centre Herbalist Building while Kenston was from The City.

"Good afternoon Herbalist Evert. Kenston will be taking your place while you transport your patient and report your findings to the Council," Honor bowed to us, her green eyes holding mystery. "You will find all you need inside."

Thank you," Evert shook Honor's hand.

Kenston and Evert helped load Atheara on the train, the rest of us piled in. The train took off for the Centre. The ride was long, the sun already setting by the time it pulled into the station. I sleepily grabbed my and Atheara's things as we got out and headed to the Medical Building of the Centre.

Two potentials approached us, "Good evening, we have been instructed to show you to the visitor's suites."

"Thank you," Father responded for us. Lillith and I were both too tired to even speak.

"I will take those, Pandria," Evert pointed to Atheara's bag. I handed it off and followed the potentials to a small building off the right of the Medical Wing.

We each choose a bedroom and went to sleep quickly. The night was a dreamless sleep. In the morning, I woke up fresh and relaxed; more so than when we were staying out at the Outer Ridges.

"Good morning!" Father beamed at me. Even he seemed happier. He was scrambling eggs in our shared kitchen.

"Yum," I tried to show enthusiasm for his cooking.

"Now Pandria, even I can cook eggs."

"Yes, but are they supposed to look gray?" I suppressed a giggle. Even this action felt foreign to me.

"No," he slopped eggs onto my plate.

Lillith came wandering in, her blonde hair disheveled. "I think even I can eat your cooking this morning."

"Rough night?" I looked up at her as Father slid some eggs onto a plate for her.

"No, actually I was in a deep sleep. Still, I feel like I've run a marathon."

"We have been running around almost non-stop for a while," Father rationalized.

After we had finished the tasteless eggs I said, "We should go see how Atheara is doing today," I tipped my plate into the sink.

"You girls go on ahead. I should check in with work and get some things done while I have the chance."

I waved to him as we set out the front door. I felt strange, returning back to the Centre. I was never keen on being here when I was a student. Now, being back I felt out of place even more. I half expected to see Thomas running up to me. I didn't see him as we walked over to the Medical Center.

When we entered the crisp white building, we were greeted by a nurse, "Good morning."

"We're here to visit Atheara," I smiled at her.

"Kenston has asked for there to be no visitors for a couple of days," the nurse explained to us.

"Is she okay?" Lillith's cheerfulness fell.

"Very much so. They are running tests and don't want to be disturbed."

"What kind of tests?" I demanded.

"It's none of your business Potential," the sound of a pen clicking finalized her statement as she stormed away.

"Fantastic," muttered Lillith. "Now what?"

"Well, I suppose we could go back to the visitor area," I shrugged.

"Excuse me," a young girl pulled on my shirt.

"Yes," I turned around.

"Are you Pandria?" she squinted up at me.

"Yes."

"Master Barnsworth would like a word with you and Lillith."

"Lead the way," I motioned for her to go ahead of us.

"What do you think this is about?" Lillith whispered in my ear.

"I'm not sure. Didn't they say yesterday they might have something they needed us to look into?"

"I think they did," Lillith scrunched her eyebrows together.

We entered one of the academic buildings and into one of the lecture halls. Master Barnsworth was piling books on her desk.

"Pandria! How lovely to see you," she gave me a hug. I was confused by this warm welcome. She never showed much interest in me while I was a student.

"Hello Master Barnsworth," Lillith waved.

"Lillith, it's nice to see you as well. Thank you, Andrea, for getting them for me. You may go now," she dismissed the girl.

"How can we help you?" I pleasantly asked Master Barnsworth.

"Please, have a seat," she motioned to two

desks. We sat ourselves down, Lillith playing with her blonde hair again. "The Council has a special request of both of you. They have noticed an increase in the number of potentials who show signs of abnormalities. They would like you to go to a Special Medical Unit and explore what might be causing the increase in these abnormalities. You are to report what you see only, nothing more. You are to interview the patients there so we might get a better idea if there is a pattern."

"Why us?" Lillith blurted.

"Both of you have experienced your own gifts transform you. Both of you have also been working on your research skills looking for the lost science group, and your Mother of course Pandria," she nodded towards me. "The Council think you would be able to provide some insight others may not. Maybe even see things we are missing because of your unique circumstances."

"Where is this Medical Unit?" I asked.

"In the City."

"What about Atheara?" Lillith sat forward in her chair.

"We are making sure Atheara is well taken care of."

"What tests are they running?" I interjected.

"Enough, both of you. The Council knows what they are doing. It is time you learn how to follow instructions rather than question them all the time," Barnsworth snapped a little more than she intended.

Lillith sat, fuming. I pondered her words and felt there was more fear behind them than anything else. I shook my head at Lillith. I was beginning to learn when she was about to rant against something she didn't agree with. This was a fight I didn't think we should have. Lillith glared at me, angry. I could put up with this dictatorship type of behavior, Lillith's nature was not so fortunate.

"Good," Barnsworth took our silence as consent to the assignment.

"When do we leave?" I asked, fighting against the words I really wanted to say.

"Tomorrow would be sufficient," she said as she got up. Barnsworth headed towards the door, a direct message stating the meeting was over.

As soon as we exited Lillith turned to face me, "Why did you accept this insane assignment?"

"What choice did we have?"

"We could have questioned it more!"

"And what would that have accomplished?

They are already set on sending us out, maybe even getting us as far from Atheara as possible. You know Atheara wouldn't want us to fight against the Masters or the Council because of her."

Lillith yanked on her hair, "Yes, but we should be questioning their motives."

"I don't disagree with you, Lillith. I do question their motives. We should see this through. Aren't you at least a little curious as to why more potentials are showing signs of defects when they use their gifts?"

"And what about your Mother?" Lillith retorted.

"We can't continue our search without Atheara. Until they are willing and able to release her, we have to wait. Not that I like it," I grumbled. A tear sneaked down the side of my cheek. I hastily scrubbed it away.

Lillith placed a hand softly upon my shoulder, "Sorry, Pandria. I should have realized how hard this waiting is on you. I wasn't thinking."

"It's all right. You're right; they are acting a bit strange."

"Well, let's see how strange this really is and be done with it."

Lillith walked back to the Visitor Center. Father was already elbowing deep into his work. He was sitting in front of a computer with a string of letters and numbers in front of him. I never understood the computer codes he wrote. He was tinkering with a machine beside it.

"How is Atheara?" he didn't look up from his work.

"Don't know, they wouldn't let us see her," Lillith walked straight to her room.

"That's not good," Father looked up at me.

"She's not keen on how they are treating us," I tried to explain.

"How are they treating us?" Father asked.

"They've asked for Lilith and me to look into a hospital which seems to be full of potentials with abnormalities like ours," I sat down across from him. "And they are not letting us see Atheara who was better before we left for the Centre."

"I'm sure there is a reasonable explanation," Father began. "Even if we don't understand what the explanation is."

"I hope you're right."

"We'll be back out to search for your Mother in no time," Father tried to smile at me. I could see worry etched into his usually calm face. I smiled back at him and nodded.

"At any rate I should go to the student store and restock some of our supplies. They asked for just Lillith and I so I guess you can stay here and hold down the fort?"

"Certainly," Father went back to his work. "I will keep trying to see Atheara to make sure she is well taken care of."

"Thanks, Dad."

I walked to the Student Store. They didn't hold a lot of items there. Most were suited for studying rather than a research mission. I replenished our nutrients bars and stocked up on some first aid supplies. I wasn't expecting trouble. I knew if we didn't fully prepare then trouble would come finding us. I still had my money card which the Centre still deposited a fair sum in each week. I used it to pay for our supplies. I tipped everything into my shopping bag and headed out. Heading out I bumped into Kyra.

"Pandria, how nice to. . . see you," she finished.

"Nice to see you, too," I forced myself to be civil. "How are you?"

"Fine. You?"

"Fine."

"You and Thomas are still together?" I tried to sound friendly.

"No," Kyra snapped.

"Um, sorry to hear that," I looked down at the ground.

"I'm sure you are. Have a nice day," she pushed past me.

"All warm and cuddly as I remember," I said to the ground.

I walked around the Centre, trying to spot Thomas. I couldn't find him anywhere. Not even in the gym which is where he normally frequented. About noon my stomach grumbled. I gave up, heading back to the Visitor Quarters.

Father was munching on a sandwich in the living quarters. "Help yourself," he said over a mouthful of turkey.

I quickly threw together a sandwich and then sat cross legged on the couch. I pulled out my tablet and began tapping around. I looked at the layout of The City and did searches about the area. The City holds the wealthy citizens. The majority of The City has shops of the high-end sort.

There was still the Political House and the Science Building along with the Herbalist Building. There was even an entertainment section, not something you saw often in The Communities. Lillith found us working in the living quarters when she entered.

"I tried to visit Atheara again. They are still saying no visitors," Lillith sat down beside me.

"I didn't think they would have changed their minds," I tapped on my tablet.

"Did you get the supplies we need?" Lillith asked.

"Yup, in my room, for now. We can split the stuff so I'm not carrying everything," I bit my tongue. I knew better than to blurt out whatever was in my head.

"No problem," Lillith jumped up and walked into my room. I shook my head.

"One of these days I will get a handle on how to speak around her." Father shook his head.

I finished eating lunch. I stretched and checked on Lillith who had already split the supplies in half. She was stuffing it into her bag. I slid the other stuff into my own bag. I placed the tablet safely inside its designated pocket and sat down on the bed.

"What do you think they are all hiding from us?" I asked Lillith.

"I've been wondering, too. First the lady at the

mine, then the Masters and possibly the Council. Even some of the Politicians seem nervous about something. I always thought it was just the nature of their job."

"I hope we learn more on our journey to The City."

"Me too. Night," Lillith waved at me.

I curled up on my bed, staring up at the ceiling, wondering what we would encounter on our trip into The City.

The next day shone bright, a rare occasion this time of the year. I wasn't going to complain. Traveling by this weather was nicer than traveling in the pouring rain. At least we were not going to be soaked. We boarded the train. I waved at Father as the train pulled away. I faced Lillith who sat across from me.

"Tell me about the layout," Lillith crossed her arms and stretched out in her chair.

I explained the overall structure of The City and where things were located. She scoffed at the Entertainment Sector.

"Highly frivolous!" she exclaimed.

I arched my eyebrows and continued. I summarized the information I studied last night: the current Seer of The City, the basic outline of the buildings, and reminded her there were no Quadrants of The City just like our Centre. Most of the buildings were going to be close together. As I finished describing The City the train came to a stop at the Station.

"All those unloading for The City!" a mechanical voice echoed from the train speakers.

We jumped off the train and looked around. In the distance I saw a fair-haired man in his late thirties walking towards us. I nodded towards him and Lillith's gaze turned to follow. She grunted and walked over to meet him.

"Lillith and Pandria I presume," he shook our hands. "I am Brenton."

"Nice to meet you," I forced a smile on my face.

"Please, follow me. The Medical Unit is not far away."

We fell in step beside him. We approached a nondescript building nestled amongst shops of tablets, dresses, and other amenities not found in the rest of The Communities.

"Is the Council keeping this a secret from the citizens?" Lillith eyed the place skeptically.

"They don't want a panic, do they?" he looked us over. "I thought they were sending professionals to have a look."

"We have experience if that is what you are concerned about," Lillith flicked her hair.

Brenton eyed us again and opened the front door. There was a small waiting room with an ornate receptionist desk. A woman with peppered hair was manning the desk.

"Good morning Brenton," she cheerfully sang to him. "And who did you bring to us today?"

"We are not here as patients," Lillith curled her fingers into a fist.

"They are here from The Centre. Remember they told us they would be sending guests?" Brenton slid a glance at her.

"Oh yes of course!" she exclaimed. "My name is Holland if you need anything dears."

I caught Lillith making gagging faces and had to restrain myself from laughing. "Thank you, Mam."

Brenton led us to a second big room where tables were lined with fresh sheets. "This is our admittance room. We look over each of our patience before they are taken into their own room. In fact, I know this sounds silly and they probably didn't tell you, but we ask all visitors to go through a general exam to be sure they aren't bringing in any contaminants into the Medical

Unit."

I had an uneasy feeling in my stomach. Lillith must have felt the same as I. She retorted, "I think not!"

"Look, I know it's a silly burden. We must insist! I can get Barnsworth on the line for you if you want to speak to her about it."

"Fine," she slammed her bag on the ground.

We both sat on one of the tables and waited. "Would have been nice if they had mentioned this, don't you think?" I looked around. The walls were a starchy white. The ceiling shined a bright metallic.

"I think we should just grab our stuff and go. They can't keep us here."

"Who is keeping you here?" A doctor came in.

"No one," I answered for Lillith. The doctor brought over a tablet and tapped on some buttons. The doctor began examining me. She looked into my eyes and jotted some notes down. The doctor looked at the lines of my cheeks, and then took down my vitals. Lillith was next. I could tell from her expression she didn't really care much for doctors.

"Someone will be in a minute to take a sample of your blood to make sure there are no viruses or other contagions in your system."

"Fantastic," I muttered.

"Not a fan of the needles, are you?" Lillith mocked.

"You think?"

"I think this is a bit excessive, don't you?"

"Maybe. I certainly don't feel sick. I would feel awful if I got one of their patients ill."

"I suppose," Lillith shrugged.

A woman in a white outfit came in, bearing a tray. She placed it on the table beside me. After cleansing my arm and sitting up the needle she withdrew some of my blood and filled a vial. She then proceeded to Lillith.

"There, not so bad was it?" she smiled at us.

"Maybe for you," Lillith rubbed her arm.

"The doctor will be back in a moment," the nurse ignored Lillith.

"Not a fan of needles, are you?" I threw it back at Lillith.

She curled her lip at me then returned to look at her arm.

"All right girls," the doctor came back in. "If you could kindly slip these sterilized clothes over your own, we can proceed into the building," he handed both of us a set of bleached white shirts, pants, and slippers which fit over our own shoes. We were instructed to leave our bags in a locker just to the left of the Admittance Room.

We entered the main Medical Unit. The hallway was long and ran down the center of the building. Every couple feet there was a room which held two beds in each room. There were children, women, and men in each of the rooms. Every six rooms there would be a wide opening with a nurse station. Across from the nurse station was a day area where children sat playing board games with each other. There were also women sitting around talking in quiet, hushed tones. I hadn't realized how many patients were actually here.

"How many patients do you have here?" I inquired.

"20 children, 30 women, and 40 men," the doctor recited.

"That's a lot of potentials," Lillith remarked.

"We call them patients here as their gifts have been altered to the point where they are not able to control them," the Doctor explained.

"A little clinical if you ask me," Lillith's anger surfaced as it always did. I noticed the Doctor still carried his tablet with him and he jotted down notes as we walked along the corridor.

We stopped at the back of the building. "This is where we keep the more damaged patients. Those who are completely unable to use their gifts. Their transformations have been so great and terrible, they have been unable to recover. There are some who are in comas while others are in a more in a vegetative state."

"May we?" I asked as I looked into one of the rooms.

The Doctor waved his arm and then said, "If you need anything please come down to the Nurses' station. They can find me if you need anything."

"Thank you," I looked back at the Doctor who was already walking away.

I walked to the bed closest to the door. A young woman lay in the bed, her blonde hair carefully brushed away from her face. The fatras lines were etched all over her face, arms, and hands. We couldn't see her eyes as they were closed. Another patient was sitting at the far side of the room in what looked to be a very uncomfortable chair. He was staring at the door.

"Hello," I waved at him. The man didn't respond.

"Vegetable state," Lillith mouthed. I shook my

head.

I touched the woman's forehead which was burning. I looked at the monitor beside her and saw her heart was beating rapidly.

"I will go ask the nurses about it," Lillith sighed. I nodded and then looked back down at her. I breathed in deeply then let my vision relax as I followed the fatras. They crisscrossed all over the place in this room and I couldn't distinguish one from another. I felt dizzy and weak. I quickly refocused my eyes to not look directly at the fatras. I gasped for breath, trying to slow my own racing heart. The woman in the bed grabbed my arm, her fingers burning into my flesh. I bit back a scream. I knelt beside her.

"Are you all right?" She did not respond. She didn't even open her eyes.

"Madam?" I inquired again. Her hand went limp and lay unmoving on the bed. Lillith came back in.

"Pandria?" concern was in her voice.

"She grabbed my arm," I whispered.

"Seriously?" Lillith walked over to the other side of the bed. "The nurse said she hasn't moved since entering the Unit."

"What about her racing heart or fever?"

"They said she's been like this since she got here."

"What about the fatras?"

Lillith began to focus her gaze. I waved my hands at her, "Stop!"

"What?" Lillith looked at me.

"I tried it already. The fatras are everywhere. I almost passed out."

Lillith looked like she wanted to crack some wise remark. Unusually she kept whatever she wanted to say to herself. She walked over to the vegetable guy. Lillith knelt beside him feeling his pulse and looking into his blank stare. "This one is hot too. His pulse is racing."

"It's almost like the fatras are consuming energy from them," I walked over to Mr. Vegetable.

We went through all ten rooms of the more severe cases. All the patients were the same: high temps and racing heart beats. Even the children who were here suffered the same. We walked back to the Nurse's Station. "Is it alright if we hang out in the Day Room with your patients for a while?"

"Sure," a nurse whose eyes held tight, dark circles.

Three of the children were playing a dice game and we sat down beside them.

"I got four fours!" a young boy exclaimed.

"You cheated!" a little girl whimpered.

"Did not!"

"Did too!"

"Both of you stop," the third child, a girl, said with some authority. "Charlie, you know you moved the dice extra when you sit them down."

"Fine," he grumbled. "I don't like playing when you're around Kathy."

I looked at Kathy and saw her eyes were completely white. The color was completely gone from them. I sucked in my breath and bit the side of my cheek.

"It's okay," the girl Kathy turned towards me. "Not many people are used to seeing a girl without proper eyes.

"What happened?" Lillith sat down beside Kathy.

"I was born blind. My parents took me to all the doctors they could. One day I discovered I could see the fatras even without normal sight. My parents took me to the Temple. There they decided to put me here so the doctors could take care of me."

I sat on the other side of her and placed a hand on her lap. I noticed even through her clothing she was burning hot. "Have they been taking good care of you?"

She turned her head towards the Nurses' Desk and then faced me, "Yes," she smiled prettily at me. "They let us play in the Day Room, take us outside every so often and let us eat cookies before bed." Her pale face looked up at me.

"Do they run a lot of tests on you?" Lillith asked.

"We have to have checkups every day," the boy named Charlie stuck out his tongue.

"You know they are just making sure we are okay," the third girl mumbled.

"What's your name?" I looked kindly at her.

"Marian," she smiled weakly at me.

"Why are you in here?" Lillith bluntly asked.

I stared at her and shook my head. Marian answered anyway, "They aren't sure. My skin burns all the time and I'm always sick."

"I'm sorry to hear that Marian," I tried to make her feel better. Words were not going to heal whatever was ailing her.

There was an awkward silence for a minute before Kathy spoke again, "What are you guys doing here?"

"We're here to find out why so many of us have been getting sick."

"Have there been a lot of people getting sick?" Charlie's grey eyes looked up at me.

"The Council thinks so, Charlie," I said.

"Are you sick?" he countered.

"A little bit," I said. I showed him my hands and he rubbed his small hand across my own.

"Does it hurt?" he asked.

"No," I smiled at him.

"Charlie, describe them?" Kathy asked.

"There are lines, like the fatras lines we all see. They are on her hands and cheeks."

"What is it like being blind?" Lillith cocked her head towards Kathy.

"I can't see anything. Yet, it's not dark. I see the fatras all the time."

"You see them here?"

"They are a lot of them here. There are more fatras here than anywhere else."

"Do you see them around us right now?"

Kathy looked at Lillith, "Yes, they are all around you, swirling," then she turned her head at me, "Around you they are so thick I can't tell any of them apart," she looked away, blinking tears from her eyes.

"Really?" I let my sight go and looked around me. I saw the normal fatras lines darting from me, not seeing the same as the young girl. I looked at Lillith, the unspoken question hanging between us.

"Thank you for talking to us," Lillith stood up. "We should probably go visit some more patients.

"Will you come play with us sometime?" Charlie asked.

"Sure," I said.

"Not the dice game, though," Kathy stared at Charlie.

His lower lip pulled out and he scooped up the dice, shoving them into his pocket. "I don't want to play this game with you around anyway," I heard him mumble.

We walked away from the children, feeling sad they were confined to the hospital. Several rooms down we heard an ear-piercing scream. I ran, Lillith not far from me. I flung open the door to find a woman of mid age pulling at her hair and hollering. I tried to grab her arms to get her to look at me. All it did was make her scream even louder. A doctor came running in with a couple of nurses.

"Please, let us handle this."

"What's wrong with her?"

"Please, back away," the nurses shoved us out of the room.

We watched from the doorway. The doctor had a needle which he was fighting to insert into her arm. The nurses had her pinned against the wall. The doctor was finally successful and injected the milky liquid into her arm. She immediately went limp. The doctor and nurses carried her to the bed in the room. They were wiping sweat from their foreheads as they exited the room.

"Is she going to be okay?" I looked at the doctor intently.

"Yes," he said. "She needs rest."

"What's wrong with her?"

One of the nurses stopped and looked us up and down. Before responding she looked at the doctor who shook his head, "She hallucinates, and they overwhelm her to the point where she becomes frantic."

"Do you know what she hallucinates?"

"She isn't coherent enough most of the time to even find out," the other nurse huffed. The nurse took off for the station.

We stood outside her door, afraid to disturb her. We knew we should check it out. Lillith finally took a deep breath and walked into the room. She checked her vitals and read up on her chart which was by the doorway. I sat beside her and felt the extreme heat from her skin.

"What do you think?" I turned to Lillith.

"Her pulse is high. She has a fever just like the rest of them. They have been giving her sedatives and calming teas. Nothing seems to help control her hallucinations. She started having problems ten years ago according to the chart," I was looking over Lillith's shoulder.

"She's been here for ten years?"

"That's what this report says."

We walked out of the room. We spent the rest of the day looking over charts and examining patients. Every one of them had high temps, erratic heart beats, and some form of disorder.

Brenton met us out front of the Medical Unit

and took us to the Political House. The Political House was grand compared to the other ones we had been to. We shared a small suite with just the two rooms and a small living area. I sat down and began to type my notes for the day, writing out the observations I had seen including any notes on unusual behavior from any of the staff or residents.

"None of them seem to be from the same area so there must be another cause to this," Lillith observed. "Nor have they all visited the same places. The kids who were born with these are able to deal with the abnormalities better than the others who developed them later in life. None of them seem to share any commonality."

"They can all see the fatras which is a common factor," I said.

"What about the fever they all seem to have?"

"I think the fever is a byproduct of whatever is causing this," I recalled our lessons from biology class. "You think the fatras are causing this problem?"

"It's the only thing they all have in common besides having fevers, racing heart beats, and some kind of ailment. Or in the words of the doctors, defect."

"How can the fatras be causing this?"

"I'm not sure," I tapped my finger on the tablet. "Every time I look too deep into the fatras I have the most problems."

"The same for me," Lillith admitted. "But don't think that makes you and me the same," she pushed off from the chair and stomped to her room.

"No problem," I sighed. I flipped off the tablet and went to bed, wondering how we were supposed to figure this out without Atheara.

We spent a couple of weeks like this, stopping in to play with the kids, checking their charts, and writing down our observations. We asked them more in-depth questions about when they used their sight to follow the fatras. We discovered most of them tried not to look at them for too long. The kids complained it hurt. The older patients who were lucid enough to speak to us seemed at a loss to describe how they felt when they tried to use their talents. I fingered the Seers Fortune Stone around my neck, always thinking of Atheara and wondering if she was recovering.

By the third week Lillith became irritable at being stuck near the Medical Unit. Even I began to snap at the Seer Ambassador of The City. We both wanted to help the patients here. However, we were eager to return to our search for the science group. Finally, we were given the word directly from The Temple to present our findings to the Council in one week.

"I say we tell them the truth. Let them know we think the fatras are somehow connected to these ailments. The more people who develop the talents the more the fatras will alter our physical well-being."

"Yes, but the last part is only a guess, not based on any real facts."

"What do you want us to tell them? We have no certainty what's going on."

"Of course not!" I tried to hold back my temper. I sucked in a deep breath and counted backwards before responding. "I think we should give them the facts only. If we try to go beyond the facts, we may sound irrational. They won't take us seriously."

"And if they ask for our opinion?"

"Then I guess we give it. If we assume it's the fault of the fatras they may never release those patients. Look at the kids like Kathy who are only able to socialize with kids younger than her. I'm certain she is lonely."

"We lie?"

"I'm not saying that either," I jammed my

knuckles into my eyes.

Many hours later we had a cohesive plan outlined. We were presenting the commonalities between all the patients, including their symptoms, and wrote out the basic facts. I saved our work including all the notes I had taken over the weeks. I placed them under a shared user file The Centre had for all their Seer interns.

The train pulled up and we hopped on board, eager to be moving away from the crowded City.

"Do you think they will actually listen to us?" I looked up at Lillith whose eyes were closed.

"Maybe," she shrugged.

The rest of our journey was in quiet thought. The distance between The City and the Temple was short and we arrived before lunch. They ushered us into the Great Temple Hall before the first of the class bells rang. I used the tablet to pull up the shared folder and presented our findings to the Council who were seated in their gilded chairs in a circle around us. They were quiet throughout the presentation, only asking for clarification when needed. At the end the lights were turned back up and we both bowed to the Elders as was custom when leaving the Great Temple room.

We both looked at each other. When no questions were asked, we excused ourselves and headed out.

"Do you think they were listening at all?" I asked in bewilderment.

"Yes," Lillith said. "Some of them even looked a little shaken by our findings."

"How could you tell; they were all so quiet."

"Their eyes say a lot. Where to now?"

Father walked up to us, "Lillith, Pandria! It's so good to see you," he gave me a big hug.

"How's Atheara?" I eagerly asked.

"She's well. In fact, she is waiting for you two to join us for lunch!" he put his arm around me and walked us back to the Visitor's Center.

CHAPTER 10:
THE BARRENS

Atheara sat in a hard chair, leaning over a cafeteria table. She looked a little pale. Other than her complexion she seemed to be doing just fine. I gave her a big hug then slumped into a chair next to her.

"How are you?" I gazed into her eyes.

"Well," she smiled weakly at me. "How was your trip?"

"Uneventful," I understated. She could tell there was a story to be told but didn't pry further. Lillith brought over four sandwiches and Father precariously carried four drinks.

"Eat up," he cheerfully dug into his food.

"What's been going on while we were gone?" Lillith inquired through a mouthful of ham and cheese.

"Not much," Father sat his food down. "They only came to me today to let me know Atheara would be out of their care and was cleared to continue our search."

"Don't know much more than what I picked up from the nurses and doctors," Atheara added. "They really only focused on my care."

"Did they figure out what happened?"

"Not really. They seem to be under the impression I hit some kind of fatras block. A destiny line which was unfinished. Therefore, I took my own spirit past our limits. I was burned by doing going too far."

"Not much of an explanation, is it?" Lillith cringed.

"Did they say it was safe for you to continue using the fatras?" I looked up at her with concern.

"Yes, the Great Seers have all been in to see me. All of them feel this is an isolated event."

"We both know it's probably not true," I stared down at my lunch.

"We will be careful, Little One," she touched my hand. The coldness of her hands alarmed me. I tried to push this fear away.

"Where do we go from here?" I asked.

"I think it's time we think outside the confines

of civilization," Father looked around to all of us.

"And what, exactly, is that supposed to mean?" Lillith looked hesitantly at Father.

"The Barrens," he answered.

"There is no way anyone can live out there let alone look for someone who is not able to live out there," Lillith seethed.

"Lillith," I warned her. I saw her take a deep breath in and without speaking aloud I could tell she was counting backwards. I had some influence on her after all.

"Father, I want to find Mother too. What you are suggesting is highly dangerous."

Atheara looked thoughtful for a woman who was recovering from an illness. I could tell she was flipping his idea around in her own mind. Finally, she responded, "I think Mr. Arturas is right, Little One. We have tried where they were last located. If they were anywhere in the City or any of The Communities someone would have reported finding them by now. I think it's time we try something drastic."

I bit my lip, scared. No one was known to last more than five minutes out in The Barrens. They always taught us in school The Barrens was a wasteland. I knew scientists occasionally went out with hazmat suits. They would have to come back often to recuperate and put on new gear. We were in an atmospheric bubble here in the confines of The Communities. I looked up at Lillith who quit eating. Not a good sign. The prospect of going beyond the safety of the Outer Ridge walls frightened her just as much as it did me.

"And how are we going to be able to get the necessary gear for this expedition?"

"We will need to speak to the Great Seers," Atheara answered.

I looked over at Lillith who, for the first time, had no snide remark.

Atheara entered the great Temple in the afternoon while we waited in the entryway. She came back with news, "They have approved our search and will be asking the 24th science Quadrant to supply us with the necessary equipment. We will need to check in every two hours and rotate our equipment. As long as we take the necessary precautions, we should be all right."

"That's settled," Father put his hand around my shoulder. "Look, you two don't have to do this. I understand how scary this must be. I know I'm not very happy about it either. I will do what must be done to find your Mother."

"I know," I looked up at him. "That's why I am coming with you."

"Are you sure, Pandria?"

"Yes."

"Will if Pandria's going and Atheara's going we might as well all go," Lillith stormed off for the Visitor Center.

"She doesn't have to go," Father commented.

"I've learned not to argue with her," I suppressed a grimace.

The night sped by fast as I tossed and turned. I guess the good thing about no sleep meant I didn't have to face any nightmares. When the sun came up, I was more exhausted than if I had just had the nightmares. Father didn't seem to take notice and Lillith looked about the same way I felt. Nobody commented on the dark lines surrounding my eyes. We packed up our stuff and headed for the station. The Great Seer Terry was there, waiting for us.

"Good morning," she bowed to us. "I wanted to make sure you had all you needed before heading out."

"Yes, thank you," I bowed to her.

"Pandria, a minute of your time," she motioned for me to follow her. Once we were out of earshot of the other's Great Seer Terry rounded on me, "The Council has approved this expedition. There are those of us with deep concerns."

"What concerns are those?"

"Other than the fact The Barrens are a dangerous wasteland you and Atheara have suffered greatly using your gifts. We fear we may lose you both," she looked at me with concern.

"We both understand the dangers we are facing. To find out what is going on outweighs these fears, don't you think?"

"Possibly," her shoulders dropped. "We cannot see your paths as they are blurred. Something we are not used to."

"The fatras are hidden even from the Great Council?" my voice rose.

"Hush, Pandria. This is not information we like to share with everyone," she looked over my shoulder to where Father, Atheara, and Lillith were about to board the train.

"The investigation into the Medical Unit, the disappearance of the science group, our inflections, they all add up to something bigger than just finding my Mother, doesn't it?"

"Some of us believe they are all interconnected."

"What do you ask of me, Great Seer?"

"Be vigilant. If you think either your life or of anyone in the group," she looked pointedly at Atheara, "is in danger, abort the mission and come back to the Centre. For your safety and the safety of others."

"You think the consequences go beyond us, don't you?" I narrowed my eyes.

"Possibly," she admitted. "The fatras are interconnected beyond what we even understand. Please, Pandria, be careful," she placed a gentle hand upon my shoulder. Great Seer Terry walked towards the group, waving farewell to them all. I stared after her for several minutes before boarding the train myself. I found a quiet spot away from everyone. The others were enveloped in their own thoughts. They didn't notice my muted solitude.

Trees whirled by as we raced back towards Quadrant 24. I thought upon the Great Seers words. She was concerned not only for our welfare. I believed her words to me were for the good of everyone. I looked at the fatras and saw them crisscross throughout the train. I saw the paths others were taking and the paths others had taken. I noticed what she said was true. All the fatras were interconnected in one way or another. When you pulled upon the string of one the others vibrated with it. The ripple flowed both forwards and backwards.

"We are here, Little One," I heard Atheara call to me from the other side of the train. I looked up and saw the simplistic buildings once more. I nodded and pulled my bag up over my shoulder. Father led us back to the Political House. The receptionist said we were set up in our regular rooms; there was no one to greet us this time.

"Wonder where everyone ran off to?" Father murmured.

"Maybe they were scared off," Lillith quipped.

A secretary knocked on the door as I was sitting my stuff down on my bed, "Good evening. Governor Cooley apologized for not greeting you and said he has received the request for the supplies from the Temple. He has made arrangements for them to be delivered to the Science building for you before you head out."

"We will start first thing in the morning," Lillith translated for Atheara.

"Thank you, Seer Atheara," she bowed. "Is there anything else we can help you with?"

"No, thank you," Lillith translated again.

"We can take the Quadrant 24 Main Train to the gate. I'm not sure how we will travel after we reach the main gate," Father scratched at the stubble on his chin.

"We can use the Security Tower as a home base," Lillith replied. "From there we will have to travel by foot. The reports say they had not seen the science group out their way. They could have passed through during a shift change."

"Not likely," I tried to say it under my breath. Everyone in the room looked at me. "Sorry, it just seems unlikely they wouldn't notice a group of people passing through the gate."

The sun burned bright through the window as I got dressed and ate a protein bar. I tapped the last few notes into my tablet about our current findings before joining the others in the living area.

"Ready Little One?" Atheara asked.

"Yes," I slung my pack over my shoulder.

Father approached me and gave me a hug, "I think we will find her soon."

"Me too," I looked up at him hopefully.

The train ride was as tense as the day before. None of us were ready to leave the confines of The Communities. This type of adventure was usually left to science members. The Council was desperate to find a new angle on the disappearance. Father had no knowledge on The Barrens just like the rest of us. His motivation to find

Mother was the strength we needed to carry on. The Security Gate loomed ahead of us. The gate was made of the same special metal mined in the hills. The locking mechanism was a simple switch and lever hydraulic system. The towers on either side of the gate loomed taller than the wall itself. The train pulled to a stop just outside the first tower. We exited the train only to be welcomed by an overwhelming heat. We quickly entered the tower to temporarily escape the heat.

"Good day. You must be Master Atheara, Potential Lilith," Security Lead Drayton shook each of our hands, "Potential Pandria, and Mr. Arturas."

"Good morning," Lillith translated for Atheara again. "Thank you for your hospitality. We are eager to begin our search and have brought with us the necessary supplies. The gentleman on the train helped us unload the freights. If we could have your assistance in bringing them in, we would be grateful."

"Of course, Potential Lillith, Master Atheara," he nodded to her as well. He motioned for two of his men to go out and haul in the cargo freights. While they brought in the equipment, he showed us to our temporary lodgings.

"As you can see these towers were built only for temporary living as we rotate shifts. The guards stay for only a couple of days at a time. We have modified this as best we could, adding more beds for all of you to fit comfortably."

"We appreciate it Captain," Lillith said. Atheara smiled at him.

I put down my bag and walked back to where the guards had set our supplies. I rummaged through the supplies. I took an inventory of everything the science building had kindly given us.

"We should head out soon. Much longer and the heat may be too much for us."

"Agreed," Lillith bit at her lower lip.

We donned suits and piled radiation pills, water, and other survival essentials into our bags. I wouldn't be able to take my tablet with me as the radiation levels would fry any electronics not outfitted for such intense heat. They did supply us with monitoring watches which allowed us to communicate with each other and keep tabs on our vital signs. The guards gave us concerned looks as we stood before the gates.

"Are you sure about this?" Drayton inquired.

"We are ready, Sir," Lillith's anger was bubbling up again.

The gate slid up. We walked out into The Barrens. The glare of the sun blinded us at first. The visor on my helmet adjusted its light sensitivity as we walked out in the arid heat.

"Search along the perimeter of the wall first, see if we notice any recent signs of others traveling around here," Atheara instructed. I relayed the message to Father who mutely nodded.

The Barrens were a living nightmare. Not even the occasional tuft of grass could be seen. Heat radiated from the rocks causing us to see visions of waves bounce off the ground. I looked towards the sky. With the special visor I could look at the sky without too much trouble but even then, I had to tilt my head down every few seconds. The solar flares from the sun seem to lick the edge of our damaged atmosphere. Every so often my watch beeped at me to let me know to adjust the radiation settings on my suit.

After searching for what seemed to be an eternity, I finally noticed some medical radios lying on the ground. I picked them up, Lillith looking over my shoulder.

"Says Quadrant 24," she pointed at the side of the radio.

"Could be the science group," I flipped it over. I looked for any other identifying marks.

"There's no plant life out here. Not even any signs of water," Lillith looked around. Heat waves rolled off the ground, obscuring our vision beyond the area we were looking. Atheara and Father walked up beside us.

"I found this pack not too far from here," Father held a tattered bag. "We should take this stuff back to the tower."

"We will need to put those in these radiation bags for decontamination," Atheara opened the bag. I slid the radio into it and Father added the bag. I tapped my watch. The monitor read my heartbeat. My heart had accelerated since we started searching out here. Atheara nodded and pointed back to the gate.

Lillith headed back to the entrance and the rest of us followed in her wake. By the time we got back to the gate sweat was pouring down the inside of my suite, making my arms and neck itch. Lillith tapped a code into a heat resistant panel. We waited for the gate to open.

As soon as we entered the gate, I felt the air become a bit cooler once it was closed. I slid the helmet off the suit and wiped my hand across my forehead.

"At least we found something," I commented.

"We need to head to the quarantine area just on the other side before we enter the tower," Atheara pointed to the right. As we approached, I noticed the small, stone building offset from the tower on the right side.

We entered the building which was cool. Being inside the building made me shiver after being out in the heat. "Your body will adjust," a guard chuckled.

"Not likely," Lillith scowled.

We were sprayed down with hoses while still in our suits. We hung the suits up on pegs to dry. We used private showers to wash down. Even though we wore suits it was best to shower to be certain all contaminants were washed away.

I dried my hair with a towel and walked back out to the main area. The bag we put the stuff in was in a chamber, decompressing. The items had been placed in a chamber which held an air gas sanitizer. Then all the air was sucked out which then filtered back out the other side of the wall.

"They are ready," Atheara pulled the items out of the chamber. She pulled them out and handed me the bag while she looked at the radio. The only words I could see on it were the 24th Quadrant. The rest had probably been weathered away from the harsh elements of The Barrens.

Atheara had better luck, "There is a high heat resistant tablet in here and some notebooks. They look rather scorched."

"Probably from the heat," Lillith observed.

Atheara managed to turn on the tablet. The logo on the opening screen said "Quadrant 24th Science Division."

"This must have belonged to someone in the group!" I got excited.

"They must have been following some lead," Father looked puzzled.

The screen popped up with various folders on the desktop. One read vegetation and another growth rate. I didn't understand the scientific terms in the notes Atheara was scanning.

"Looks like they found a connection between the plant life along the edge of the Wall to the plants in the hills of the Outer Ridges," Atheara surmised.

"You can understand this rubbish?" Lillith glared at the screen.

"Some of it," Atheara flipped to the next set of notes. "I remember some of it from my regular Academics training."

"I think, Mr. Arturas, you should take these back to where we are staying and contact one of the scientists who are still left in the 24th Quadrant. Pandria, Lillith, and I will go back out to see if we can follow the fatras while we are out there," Lillith communicated for Atheara.

"Do you think it's safe?" I looked at her with alarm.

"What choice do we have?" Atheara shrugged.

"Maybe Pandria's right on this one, Atheara," Father looked at her with concern.

"Do you have another suggestion?" Atheara asked.

"I think we should go back out and search one more time. We need to see if there is something we missed. If we can't find more evidence, then we will go with your suggested route. For now, I think investigation is a much safer option," Father looked up hopefully.

Atheara nodded. We adorned new suits for a trip back out in The Barrens. All we found was harsh sand blowing into our masks constantly. After searching for a couple more hours, we called it quits as the sun began to sink back towards the ground.

I huffed as we went through the same process we went through earlier. We wandered back to the Tower. After four attempts Father reached someone in the science building. He returned to our temporary living quarters.

"They will be sending someone out first thing in the morning," he sat down across from me.

"Any luck, Pandria?"

I tapped on the tablet and looked through the detailed notes. There were sketches of plant life, radiation levels, and other notes on the acrid climate of The Barrens. "Nothing more than what we have noted earlier. They had made notes about the plant life they found in the Outer Ridges and were trying to produce a more radioactive resistant plant to transplant to The Barrens."

"Any success?" Lillith quietly asked.

"No," I responded quickly.

The head guard came in, "How is everything?"

"Just fine," I replied for Atheara. "We are stopping for today."

"Good. We don't typically let anyone out at night."

"Why?" Lillith asked.

"Dangerous toxin levels in the ground radiate up at night. Who knows what kind of dangerous creature has evolved out there," he looked shaken.

"Thank you," Father took pity on him. "We appreciate your cooperation."

"I hope the things you collected may help you

find your wife, Mr. Arturas."

"I hope so, too."

We were left alone. On the other side of the tower, I could hear the lower murmur of voices from the night guards. I couldn't make out what they were saying. My face felt burnt after a day trudging through The Barrens. Even with the suit someone could still get a serious tan spending any time on the other side of the wall.

Father sat munching on some carrots while I read entries to him. "This one says they had found a cross species of plant which grows in intense heat. They were having trouble overcoming the radiation levels for any prolonged amount of time," I swiped the note aside and opened another file. "This one says they have planted bitters, pepper type plants, and something called mallions, but they were unable to live longer than a week."

"Do they say anything about why the guard didn't know they had gone out the gate?" Lillith scathingly inquired.

"No," I kept my answer short to prevent a fight. It was a struggle to not roll my eyes at her.

Atheara sat cross legged from me, searching through all the pockets in the bag. She pulled out a necklace that looked like the Fate necklace she had given me. "I don't recall a Seer going with the group," I slid off my cot and onto hers. I fingered the jewel with curiosity. Just as I did an image flashed through my mind. The speed was so quick I wasn't able to make out what I was seeing.

"What is it, Little One?" Atheara held my hand.

"I don't know," I stuttered. "I thought I saw images but couldn't make them out."

Lillith walked over to us and handled the necklace. "Feels cold," she said. "I don't see any images."

"Why would this necklace be cold and the items so hot from being out there in The Barrens?"

"Another puzzle to our list which seems to be growing," Father rubbed at his head.

"A lot of questions with no answers," Atheara agreed.

We were all so exhausted. We didn't really eat anything more than a ration bar. I sleepily laid on the bed. I fell asleep while fingering the necklace Atheara gave me. I tried to recall the images which had passed before me but couldn't. I was frustrated. The memories were hard to remember and were just out of my reach, teasing me.

Sleep was rough. We were all feeling the residual heat of The Barrens. The science person from Quadrant 24 arrived before the sun rose.

"Good morning," she cordially greeted us. "My name is Laurel."

"Nice to meet you, Laurel," Father shook her small hands.

"I understand you found something belonging to the 24th Science Quadrant?"

"Yes, please follow me," Father escorted her to our rooms.

I grabbed the notebook and tablet. They were cooler than yesterday. Heat still radiated from them. "We found these just outside the gate."

"The notebooks are rather bad, aren't they?" Laurel flipped through the notebook. "The writing is very difficult to read. Parts are missing due to contamination. She then flipped on the tablet. She scanned the front screen and typed a series of letters and numbers, being denied each time. "This will take a bit longer to crack than I had hoped."

"We will leave you to it then?" Father nodded towards the kitchen.

Atheara, Lillith, and I followed him. "I think I should stay here and watch over her."

"You don't trust her?" Lillith cocked her head to the side.

"No," the answer slid out from him. He rolled his eyes and grunted. "I mean, we don't really know her. Obviously, something is going on here."

"Agreed," I answered for Atheara. "Atheara thinks it's time we tried the fatras in The Barrens."

"I don't know. It seems dangerous every time you guys try."

I looked at Father, knowing convincing him would be difficult. "Dad," I stepped towards him, "You and I both want to find Mother. I know it's been difficult, lately, looking at the fatras past The Communities. We have to try. If we don't and realize later following them could have steered us to her, we would regret it."

"She would never forgive me if I lose you to find her."

"You won't," I assured him.

"You don't know that, Pandria."

"Often in life we have to let go the things we love most in order to let them grow," Lillith translated.

Father scratched the stubble on his face. "I don't like this. If Atheara thinks it necessary, then who am I to argue?"

I gave Father a big hug, burying my face into his chest. "Thank you, Dad."

He nodded and then walked back into the common room. I could hear Laurel ask, "Is everything okay?"

I didn't hear his response because Lillith stated, "Maybe we should get going before it gets too hot."

I nodded and we packed our gear. We walked to the outer building suiting up once again. The morning Guard let us out the gate. We walked close to the wall where we had found the science stuff. The ground would be too hot to sit on. We stood shoulder to shoulder, letting our sight go and following the fatras. They were brighter than what we normally saw. Just before we hit the fiery wall, which was not far from where we were standing, we pulled up short. I could hear Atheara's voice in my head. "It ends."

"Yes, but why?" I responded back in my head.

"Not sure."

"I see Mother's familiar aura here right where we are standing. Then it burns up in the divide.

In fact, the fatras seem all tangled here."

"Lillith is getting sick from the tangled mess of fatras."

"Is she going to be alright?"

"Yes," Atheara responded.

"I think I can make out Mother's line amongst the chaos. I reached out just a little further with my mind."

"Careful Little One," Atheara warned.

"It's like a rope which is all tied up and knotted," I observed. "If I could just get it detangled, I could find her."

"Detangling a fatras line has never been done before. We don't know what the consequences would be. We simply follow the lines to go around the tangles," Atheara warned.

"I have to try," I forcefully pushed Atheara out of my thoughts.

There wasn't any sound. I shut her out and was alone in the vast wasteland. I felt the searing heat. I knew I could do this. I gently tugged on a fatras line, testing it. I felt the reverberating shake through all the lines. I didn't want to pull so hard the line broke. I would lose her forever.

"Stop!" Atheara warned. I could hear Lillith

breathing hard over the microphone. "We need to get Lillith back to safety."

I pushed Atheara's voice away from me again, isolating myself from her and Lillith. Breaking a fatras line would not be a good thing. I gritted my teeth and could feel sweat start to pour down my face. I willed the fatras lines around her aura to separate, carefully pulling lines off of each other.

I heard Atheara's faint voice, "Pandria, this has never been done before. We have always read the lines, not manipulate them like you are doing right now. Stop," her voice warned.

"I can do this!"

I shut her out of my mind once more. I re-focused on the lines around Mother's fatras line, reeling it back in towards me. I felt it snag and saw the lines pull tight into the Divide. "Mother!" I called out in my mind. I heard her voice ghostly echo back to me, giving me hope. I pulled harder on her line. Like a rubber band it shot into me. I fell and then there was blackness.

CHAPTER 11: HOME

I felt a cool touch to my forehead which burned. My eyes watered even though they were closed. I didn't want to open my eyes. The searing pain was almost to the point of being unbearable. I moaned and I heard a hushed whisper close to my ringing ears.

"Sleep now," I thought I heard my Mother whisper. Then she sang her beautiful lullaby. The notes soothed me back into the void of a dreamless slumber.

The next I woke I was able to open my eyes. The burning pain still enveloped all my senses. "Rest Little One," I heard Atheara.

"Mother," I groaned.

"You must rest," Atheara commanded.

"Is she here?" I balled my hands into fists, clenching the starchy sheets in my hands.

"Yes," I heard Atheara respond before I passed

out again.

The last I woke I was in a stark white room. I could hear the beep of a monitor near me. I slowly turned my head, the world spinning with just the slightest movement.

"Good morning sleepy head," Father chuckled.

"Dad," I said through cracked, dry lips.

"Sip this," he instructed.

It took all my strength to sip the sweetened water. I felt it cool me from the inside out. The walls stopped moving. I looked at Father. "Where am I?"

"The hospital in the Centre," he held my hand.

"What happened?" my voice cracked.

"You found her," Father smiled at me.

"She's here?" I tried to sit up. I immediately regretted it. I felt the blood drain from my face. Father jumped up from his chair and helped me lay my head back down on the cool pillow.

"She's resting right now. She will come back in a little bit, Pandria," Father assured me.

"The scientists who were with her?"

"Back as well."

"Are they okay?" I smacked my lips together. I

felt Father tip more liquid into my mouth. I tried not to choke on it.

"Yes," he said. "Now sleep."

I wasn't in a position to argue with him. Without my permission my eyes closed.

I woke up again to see Lillith's face scanning a tablet. "Standing guard?" I tried not to laugh.

"Do you plan on doing any more stupid acts of courage?" she didn't look up from her reading.

"Not any time soon," I slowly stretched.

"Then no, I'm not guarding," she snapped the computer shut.

I laughed and instantly regretted it. All my muscles felt like they had been stretched beyond their capacity. "Don't do that?" I grumbled.

"What, make you laugh?" Lillith stood up.

"Yes," I held my sore stomach.

"Hey, it's not my fault you went and manipulated something beyond your ability," Lillith checked the vitals machine. I coughed. I felt the dryness in my throat. Lillith tipped cooling liquid into my mouth.

"What is that stuff," I stuck out my tongue after swallowing.

"Not sure, really," Lillith swished the liquid around in the cup.

"You could be giving me poison for all I know," I looked at her.

"I would have poisoned you long ago if I was going to do that," Lillith sat back down.

"Where is everyone?" I asked.

"Atheara is reporting to the Great Seers. Your Father is attending to your Mother. As you can see, I'm babysitting."

"Nice," I grumbled.

I pulled myself stiffly up into a sitting position.

"Whoa there," Lillith tried to push me back down. "I don't want to be fired from this job."

"Didn't know you liked babysitting so much," I sarcastically replied.

"Better than listening to whining students in boring classes," Lillith retorted.

"I'm glad to know I am better than classes."

"Feel special?" Lillith grin.

"Every day," I smiled back.

Lillith filled me in on what happened. She

wasn't even sure what I had done to bring back the missing group. She had seen all the fatras in a tangled chaotic mess. She had withdrawn from it to resist being swallowed whole by them. She said she had started feeling sick and Atheara had been trying to get me to agree to go back to the gate. The next thing she knew I collapsed to the ground in a flash of bright light. Atheara had rushed to my side and used her own gifts in the fatras to untangle me from the lines which surrounded me. Seeing the fatras lines tangled around a person like that was nothing she had ever seen before. Atheara was afraid she wouldn't be able to do it.

Lillith said she noticed a group of people near the gate. They were all lying on the ground, unconscious. Lillith had gone to the gate and called for assistance. She helped bring everyone back to The Outer Ridges. Lillith said the Security Force raced us back to the Centre. With the power of all the combined Great Seers and various herbalists they were able to heal me to the point where they didn't fear for my life.

"What about Mother?" I looked at her hopefully.

"They say she is making a full recovery. None of the scientist group is sure what happened. They had exited the gate late at night when no one was around. They were often permitted the privilege, according to your Mother, to exit without Guard assistance. The next thing they knew they were back at the gate being carried inside."

"What has The Great Seers said about this?" I lay my hands flat on the bed.

"They are concerned you took an uncalculated risk," Lillith came straight to the point. One of the things I was beginning to admire about her.

"Did they say if they are going to kick me out of the Seers?"

"I don't think so. I had the sense they didn't want either of us back in the Centre, though. They were angry, Pandria. The Elders said they had warned you to do what was best for everyone. Instead, you violated our laws of physically altering the fatras lines. You did something that has never been done before. Everyone is worried about the consequences."

"I wonder why they didn't kick me out then," I pondered this thought. We were both silent for a long time. After a while Lillith went back to her reading. I lay in bed, staring at the ceiling. Hours later Atheara entered the room.

"You're awake, Little One!" she beamed at me.

"Yes, alive and kicking."

"Little One," She began. It was always going to

be a lecture when she started with those words. I intervened before she could get into full swing.

"I know, I took an uncalculated risk. It was wrong of me," I nodded towards Lillith who mocked me. The exchange was not lost on Atheara.

"Stop," she ordered both of us.

"Look, I would say I'm sorry, but I brought them back so I'm not going to," I tried to cross my arms. They felt so heavy at the moment. My arms just spasmed instead.

"There's no use in being stubborn with me," Atheara crossed her arms. "What you did was not just wrong because you risked your life. What you did was incredibly rare."

"No one has ever manipulated the fatras before?" I looked at her with concern.

"No, Little One, they have not."

"If it helped find the lost science group then why am I being lectured?"

"No one is denying you certainly helped in this situation. What you did was unprecedented. The Council, they are scared of what you can do."

"Are you?" I looked up at my lifelong mentor.

She looked shaken at first. Then resolve won

over, "No."

"When do you think I can get out of here?" I changed the subject.

"It will be a while," Lillith put down her tablet again.

"Ugh," I said.

"She has no idea, does she?" Lillith turned to Atheara.

"I think not," I heard Atheara respond to her.

"What do you mean?" panic rose in my voice.

"Settle down," Lillith sighed. She walked over to a sink on the far side of the room. She brought back with her a handheld mirror.

"What?" I gave her a confused look.

"Just look," Lillith sat back down in her chair.

I stared at the reflection in the mirror. It took me a minute to realize the person I was looking at was me. The lines which had adorned my hands, cheeks, and eyes were etched everywhere. They swirled with a golden line written with a fine tipped pen. I would have thought it beautiful except it covered my entire face. I looked down at my hands and noticed the lines were also covering both arms. I began searching all around. I realized it was on my entire body.

"What?" I looked wide eyed at Atheara.

"Did this happen when I pulled apart the fatras?"

"Yes," Atheara replied.

I lay back down on the pillow and slid the mirror away from me. Lillith looked at Atheara. They both left the room.

I must have fallen asleep. When I opened my eyes again Mother was sitting by me, stroking my hair away from my face. She looked like I remembered except her complexion was paler than normal.

"Mother!" I exclaimed and slid out of bed to give her a hug. The room lurched but I was able to manage it.

"I'm here, Pandria," Mother hugged me back.

She helped me lay back down. "Pandria what you did was very brave, but you must be careful."

"You would have done the same for me," I tried to defend myself.

"Yes," she admitted. "You could have done more harm than good."

"What happened?" I asked her.

"I'm not sure. I've been trying to recall what

happened. It's like grasping at an imaginary object. I think it's there. Then it disappears the moment I try to grab it."

"How are your colleagues?"

"They are mending just like me."

"Are you okay?" I scrunched my eyebrows together.

"I think so," Mother patted my hand. "There are days where I feel lost and confused, out of sorts. Other days I feel grounded."

"Lost?" I sat up again. "You're here, with us. You're home."

She smiled at me, "Yes, thanks to you."

I smiled back at her. I laid my head back down on the pillow, just staring at her. I didn't want to close my eyes in fear of waking to find Mother would be missing again. Mother started singing the lullaby and my eyes closed.

A couple weeks later the medical team released me from the hospital. To my dismay I found I had been in there for two months before even waking. I had missed a lot of my internship. I would have to start over. The Council decided it was best to let me serve in my own district, Quadrant 12. The Great Seers insisted Atheara accompany me. I was to spend at least another full month at home with my parents before returning to my Seer duties. This was a mandated condition for them to release me from the hospital. I reluctantly agreed. It was either that or stay in the boring Medical building in the Centre.

I sat on a bench on our front porch reading an article about radiation resistant plant life. I had taken an interest in Mother's work since returning from our journey to rescue her.

"Here you go," Mother handed me an ice-cold drink. I couldn't stand hot drinks even in cold weather. Anything hot reminded me of the pain I endured when returning from The Barrens.

Mother sat beside me, reading from her tablet. I reflected upon my hearing with the Elders. I entered the Temple again; my resolve was solid. I was owning up to what I did. I didn't know if they were right or not. Perhaps there would be consequences more dire than a group of missing scientists. I had also felt helping people was more important than any consequence.

"Do you know what you have done?" Elder Jaemson scowled at me from behind his red hair. "How dare you endanger everyone in The Community like that!" his voice growled. His grey eyes pierced through me. I was afraid I was going to lose my resolve.

"Peace, Elder Jaemson," Terry eyed me cautiously. "What is done is done. We cannot go back and undo it. If we did, we could make things even worse."

"I don't regret saving those people," I stood my ground. I saw dismay on Atheara's face. Uncharacteristically she was quiet. She would usually berate me for being so obstinate.

Elder Jaemson sighed and closed his eyes. "The Elders have decided to keep you as an intern. However, let this be a warning to you. You must not defy our laws again or the consequences will be dire for both you and your family."

I started to speak out against him again. Atheara curtly nodded no to me. If I defied the Elders, life could become much worse for my parents. Even if my actions were right in saving my Mother and the science group, I could do much more harm to everyone else. I understood their concerns. I wasn't going to apologize for my actions. I clenched my fists into tight balls and bowed, "Thank you Elder Jaemson." I turned away and started walking towards the door.

Elder Jaemson's voice floated back to me, seething, "I will use any reason to kick you out and leave you for the Barrens to deal with if you defy us again."

Although I had heard his words I continued to

walk out of the Temple, not letting his threat get to me.

I brought myself back to the present. "When do you have to return to work?" I looked at Mother.

"They are giving me another week before I return," she sat across from me.

"Do you have to go back?" worry crossed my face.

"Yes. I promise I won't be going out to The Barrens," she involuntarily shook.

"Okay, but only if you promise," I leaned back into my chair.

"Don't get too comfortable," I heard Lillith's familiar voice.

I suppressed a sigh, "Can't a medically released patient enjoy her time with her family?"

"Not when duty calls," Lillith walked up on the porch.

"What duty?" I demanded. "I thought my duty was to heal and rest up."

"You guys really need to listen to the reports more often," Lillith pulled her tablet out of a backpack strapped around her thin shoulders.

She held it towards me. I hesitantly took it.

She had the screen on a report written by The City's Political House. It read:

"Mines are continuing to disappear along with the work force mining in those areas. Scientists are trying to determine the cause of these disappearances. No plausible explanation has been issued thus far."

"More people are disappearing?" I almost shouted.

"Yes," Lillith responded.

"What about my report to the Great Seers?"

"The Council is keeping your story silent. They don't want to start a panic and have people lose the trust of the Seers."

I looked at Mother, "Did you know about this?"

"I've heard rumors," Mother avoided my gaze.

"Is there anything else you have been keeping from me?" I rounded on her.

"Don't take that tone with me," Mother warned me.

I took a deep breath and said, "Sorry, Mother. I wasn't trying to accuse you of anything."

Mother eyed me for a moment before saying, "Your Father and I were concerned about your health. We didn't want you to worry. Lillith, when are you both to report to the Political House?"

"Tomorrow afternoon," she plopped down on a chair next to me.

"Well then stay with us tonight," Mother cheerfully said. "We can have a sort of party before you guys have to go."

"Thank you, Mrs. Arturas," Lillith politely accepted.

Mother walked into the house. I could hear the clink of pots and pans as she started dinner.

"What is it?" I looked at Lillith.

"Remember the strange woman who approached us and was trying to warn us?"

"Yes."

"She's also missing."

EPILOGUE

"And why are we here?" I questioned David.

"Because they said so, Adalyn," David sounded exacerbated. "Now hush."

I stood quiet, looking out at the vast expanse of nothingness. The sun shone brighter just a mile from where we were standing. I couldn't help but to shiver in my Exon-suit. "There's nothing out there!" I stamped my foot.

"Everyone saw the flash. Something must have caused it," David raised a furry brow.

"Yea, yea," I kicked at the dirt. "We know the settlement is just over the hill. It was probably something from them."

"Yes, might be true but we should still look into it. With things disappearing out here the Nomad Tribes are getting a little anxious," David explained.

"Whatever," I turned my back to him. My Exon-suit began to click, indicating a message coming in. I clicked on the band around my wrist.

"Meet us just south of the Wall," Jack's voice came across with a lot of static.

"Why?" I demanded. David gave me an un-amused look, so I recanted, "I mean yes Sir," I pretended to salute with my free hand.

We both punched the high temperature button on our suits, and it adjusted. I could feel the cooling tubes fill with even more liquid and I stopped sweating. I checked my band again and saw the terrain had higher levels of radiation. I punched in a code which activated the adjustment of the radiation shielding liner. We hiked over the hill and came up to just south of the Wall. The co-ordinates Jack sent us beeped indicating we were within five miles of the meeting location. David scanned the hill and saw a slight shimmer to the left of us. He pointed and I saw the cooling huts in a low sand bowl. We headed over and entered the first chamber. I felt the air decompress. Jets sprayed against our suits. We entered the deployable building, taking off the top portion of our form fitting suits.

"Good afternoon, Sir?" David saluted.

"Good afternoon, David," Jack shook his hand.

"And Adalyn," he gave me a glance over, more than he had done in my whole lifetime.

"May I ask what is going on, Sir?" David looked concerned.

"That's the question of the hour," Jack waved at all the computers lining the far wall. "The Nomadic Tribes of five, nine, and twelve have disappeared off the charts. Even some of the permanent settlements have vanished without a trace."

"Is it the radiation levels?" I looked at the radiation monitor.

"No," a girl who was sitting in front of one of the computer screens swiveled around. "It's not."

"Loralee, it's wonderful to see you!" I truly became excited.

She smiled warmly at me. Her smile slid away, "We aren't sure what happened."

"What about those Seers we met a year ago? What do they say?" David looked to Jack.

"They say we've gone too far," Jack sighed. "The Fates have snapped."

"Sounds ludicrous to me," I grumbled.

"Ludicrous or not we have a serious problem," Jack ignored my anger, as always.

"Look here," Loralee swung back into her chair. She tapped a few buttons and the monitor showed just outside the Wall. The display showed a young girl falling to the ground. She was surrounded by a bright light. Then shadows engulfed the images, blocking out everything.

"They warned us," Jack crossed his arms.

"Yes, they didn't give us many details," I clenched my teeth.

"David, Adalyn, it's time. They have given us the proper clothing of those behind the Wall. They have contacted us and let us know the time and day we are to meet them at the gate. They will smuggle you in, introducing you as scientists."

"Not a difficult task," I kicked the side of Loralee's chair.

"You will need to infiltrate the very heart of their civilization. What the Seers call The Temple. You need to find a way to get us inside before we are all wiped out."

I cringed. I didn't really feel comfortable around the Seers who were helping us. I didn't really relish the idea of being around a whole tribe of them.

"When do we leave Sir?" David gazed up at his commanding officer.

"Now," Jack stated. "Sorry about the late notice, brother," Jack smiled.

"Typical," I scowled at Jack. I hated the connection these two shared. Being inducted into this group was hard enough let alone competing for the attention of one brother over another.

Loralee handed us the clothes. They were lighter than anything I had ever felt before and much smoother than our well-worn clothes. Entering private chambers, I quickly dressed and then took a scouting pack they had put together for us. I changed into my Exon-suit and slung the pack over my shoulders.

"You will have to leave those outside The Communities" Jack warned. "The Seers will get you in during the dark and take your suits just outside the gate. They will hide them the best they can. I will send a runner to pick them up."

"Yes Sir," David saluted again.

By the time we headed out the sun had already sunk low. The cooler temps began to rapidly drop. The fluid lines emptied and refilled with warm liquid. We neared the Wall. Its metallic surface was very uninviting. The gates cranked open by a crude pulley device. There they were, the Seers who our tribe had met a year ago. They had with them a woman I did not recognize. They walked over to us, indicating we should remain silent as we walked through the ominous gate. We hesitantly took off the suits. The Seers left through the gate once more.

The woman took off her own suit. She was older than David and me. She wore a white shirt and gray slacks. When the Seers returned, she looked equally uncomfortable as I felt but I didn't say anything.

"Welcome to the Outer Ridges," one of the Seers shook David's hand. "We've been expecting you. This is Margaret. She is one of the leaders of the group who has been trying to warn the Seers of our peril."

"And let me guess," I responded, "they don't believe her."

"That is correct," Margaret's voice rasped. "But I

believe we have a way to convince them."

"And how do we do that?" David politely asked.

"We need to find a young girl by the name of Pandria."

ACKNOWLEDGE-MENT

I would like to thank my husband, Jamison, who has always believed I have had a story worth telling, my parents Ron and Deby Ward who have always encouraged me to reach for the stars, my brothers Dean and Jeremi, the Ward, Johansen, Burkhart, and Vanderhoof family who have always supported us no matter where in the world we are, and my friends who have become family. Without you all I wouldn't be where I am today. Thank you so much for all you have all done for us over the years.

ABOUT THE AUTHOR

Teresa Vanderhoof

My name is Teresa Vanderhoof. I have worked in the field of education for 12 years. Although certified as a Music Eductor I have had the priveledge to work as a substitute teacher and a para educator over the years as we travel around the world. Even as a middle school student I was interested in teaching. Working with students has been a point of inspiration for me. I have combined my love of working with kids and creating new worlds to publish my first book, "Seer's Fortune" which is book 1 of Seer's Trilogy. While writing this book I used my experience from my years in education to develop my characters. I created obstacles which, in some ways, reflect the obstacles I have seen students face as they learn how to cope with their own growing pains.

BOOKS IN THIS SERIES

Seer's Trilogy

The world has been left in ruins by The Great War. The Seer's have used their abilities to see into the present, past, and future to create peace. Pandria Arturas is brought up in this new world. Growing up is challenge enough but to also be responsible for the fate of the world is even more demanding. Their world starts falling apart and it's up to her to save them all.

Seer's Fortune

All Pandria Arturas wanted was to be like her Mother and Father, to continue to study the sciences. Instead, she was ushered into the Seer ranks, the heart and salvation of The Communities. From birth she was taught that to be a Seer was an honor as they guide society by reading the lines of fate. They do this in order to avoid conflict and prevent a war like the Nuclear War which devastated their world. As Pandria trains to become a coveted Seer she begins to question if the Seers have over manipulated the lines of Fate. This conflict resides within her as she looks for a group of missing scientists, her mother amongst them. She either has to learn to accept the consequences of her "gift" or lose her mother forever.

Seer's Folly

Pandria has successfully rescued her mother and the science group. However, did her choice to save them come at a price? She races against time as she works with Lillith to discover why parts of The Communities are mysteriously disappearing. Every time she uses her gift, there seems to be a price. Who can she turn to in her time of need?

Seer's Fate

War is imminent. Fear and misunderstanding are threatening to destroy the world once again. People are disappearing and bits of their world are being lost to the unknown. Each side blames the other. No one knows the pain of the loss of a loved one better than David and Lillith who have lost their friend Pandria to The Void. She is the hope and key to bring back those who have mysteriously disappeared. Can Pandria Arturas stop this war before it completely destroys everything they have all worked so hard to rebuild after the last Great War? Join David and Lillith as they race against time to save their beloved friend from being lost in the endless Void for eternity. Discover what the new Seer's Fate will be. The epic conclusion to the Seer's Trilogy.

Printed in Great Britain
by Amazon